A JAR OF
DREAMS

DATE DUE

DATE DUE		
NOV 03 1989		
NOV 5		
NOV 12 '90		
DEC 10 '90		
MAR 18 '91		
MAY 9 '91		
MAY 20 '91		

GAYLORD   PRINTED IN U.S.A.

BY THE SAME AUTHOR

The Dancing Kettle
The Magic Listening Cap
Takao and Grandfather's Sword
The Promised Year
Mik and the Prowler
Rokubei and the Thousand Rice Bowls
The Forever Christmas Tree
Sumi's Prize
Sumi's Special Happening
Sumi and the Goat and the Tokyo Express
The Sea of Gold
In-Between Miya
Hisako's Mysteries
Journey to Topaz
Samurai of Gold Hill
The Birthday Visitor
The Rooster Who Understood Japanese

Journey Home
(A Margaret K. McElderry Book)

A JAR OF
DREAMS

Yoshiko
Uchida

A Margaret K. McElderry Book

AN ALADDIN BOOK
Atheneum

Published by Atheneum
All rights reserved
Copyright © 1981 by Yoshiko Uchida
Published simultaneously in Canada by McClelland & Stewart, Ltd.
Composition by American-Stratford Graphic Services, Inc.
Brattleboro, Vermont
Manufactured by Fairfield Graphics
Fairfield, Pennsylvania
ISBN 0-689-71041-0
First Aladdin Edition

For my California cousins

A JAR OF
DREAMS

I

◆━◆━◆━◆━◆━◆━◆━◆━◆━◆━◆━◆━◆━◆━◆━◆━◆━◆━◆━◆

I NEVER THOUGHT ONE SMALL LADY FROM JA-
pan could make such a big difference in my life, but
she did. I'm talking about my Aunt Waka who came to
visit us the summer a lot of things changed in our
house, including me.

That summer turned special from the day Mama
got the letter that caused her strange behavior. It was
on a Tuesday, one of the days Mama went to work
for Mrs. Phillips to clean her house and scrub her
floors. The minute I got home from school and walked
into the kitchen, I knew something was wrong. Well,
not wrong exactly, but strange. I felt the way I do
when I've got one sweater button in the wrong hole
or when I put my left slipper on my right foot.

In the first place, water was dripping from the
kitchen faucet and splashing on dishes Mama had
left in the sink. Ordinarily Mama never leaves the
house without checking the faucets to see that they're

3

turned off good and tight. And she never leaves dirty dishes sitting in the sink when she goes to work.

But that wasn't all. She'd left so many things scattered over the kitchen table, I couldn't even see the yellow oilcloth cover. The Japanese newspaper was spread out on the table with a square hole in it where Mama had cut out the recipe for the day. And she hadn't even bothered to put away the scissors she'd used. There were two or three bills Mama hadn't opened and a five-page letter from Japan that hadn't been put back in its envelope. The table was a mess, and if I had left it that way, or my little brother, Joji, we sure would have heard about it from Mama.

I looked at the Japanese writing in the letter, squiggling up and down the soft rice paper like a lot of skinny black spiders, and wished I could read it. But of course I couldn't, because I don't study very hard at Japanese Language School, and besides I'm not far enough advanced to read that kind of writing. All I could read were the numbers that said, first day of the fifth month, 1935. I had a hunch, though, that whatever was in the letter was the reason Mama had gone off acting like Joji instead of her own neat self. And I couldn't bear to wait until she got home to tell me what was in the letter.

I stuffed the letter in the envelope, grabbed an apple from the bin in the sunporch, and headed for Papa's barbershop. It was a hot day, but I ran all the way to Shattuck Avenue and forgot to wait until I'd gotten to Channing Way before crossing Shattuck. That meant I'd have to walk by the Starr Laundry, which I usually avoid like a nest of cobras because of Mr. Wilbur J. Starr, the owner.

The reason I hate and despise Wilbur J. Starr is because he is so mean and nasty. Once when I was in the fourth grade, Joji and I walked by his laundry on the way home from Papa's shop. Old Wilbur J. Starr was standing in the doorway of his laundry, and when Joji and I walked by minding our own business, he yelled, "Get outta here you damn Jap kids!"

Joji dropped my hand and began to run. "Come on, Rinko," he yelled. "He's gonna git us." And he went steaming on ahead of me, pounding hard on his fat little legs.

I wanted to run with him, but when I heard Wilbur Starr laughing behind us, I just held up my head and said to Joji, "Pretend you never heard him." But my knees were shaking so hard, I could barely walk home.

Ever since that day, I try never to walk by the Starr Laundry if I can help it, because I hated the way I felt when Wilbur Starr called me a Jap. It made me really mad, but it also made me feel as though I was no good. I felt ashamed of who I was and wished I could shrink right down and disappear into the sidewalk.

There are a few white girls in my class at school

who make me feel that way too. They never call me "Ching Chong Chinaman" or "Jap" the way some of the boys do, but they have other ways of being mean. They talk to each other, but they talk over and around and right through me like I was a pane of glass. And that makes me feel like a big nothing. Some days I feel so left out, I hate my black hair and my Japanese face. I hate having a name like Rinko Tsujimura that nobody can pronounce or remember. And more than anything, I wish I could just be like everybody else.

It would be wonderful if my best friend, Tami Nukaga, could be in my class so I'd at least have one friend at school. But when our old school was closed because it wasn't earthquakeproof, we were split up and sent to different schools. So now I go to Madison, where most of the kids are white and live in the nice houses up in the Berkeley hills.

I never would have made the mistake of crossing Shattuck Avenue too soon that afternoon, if I hadn't been so busy thinking about the letter. But since I had, I just turned my head when I passed the Starr Laundry so I wouldn't see Mr. Starr if he was standing at the counter. I got a whiff of hot irons steaming on damp cloth as I went by, and I thought a few mean thoughts. I hoped some of the pressers were burning fuzzy brown holes in the shirts and sheets. It would serve Wilbur Starr right.

I turned up Channing Way and went past Uncle Kanda's dry cleaning shop. He isn't really my uncle. He's one of Papa's best friends since they came over from Japan together on the same ship, and he comes to our house every single Sunday of the year. In fact, it wouldn't feel like Sunday if Uncle Kanda didn't come.

I was ready to wave and holler at him as I went by, but I guess he was in back at his sewing machine mending clothes or maybe tailoring a suit to make a little extra money. Mama says Uncle Kanda is the best tailor in Berkeley and sews better than any woman she knows.

When I got to Papa's barbershop, I pushed open the door with the gold lettering that said, "Shintaro Tsujimura, First Class Barber," and heard the little bell ring over my head. There was no sign of Papa, and his two barber chairs were empty. But I knew where to find him. He'd be out in the lot behind his shop working on somebody's car. If Papa had his way, he would be a mechanic or repairman. He'd probably spend every minute of the day working on anything that needed fixing and read "Popular Mechanics" in his spare time.

Papa says some day, when he's paid up all his debts, he's going to get rid of the barbershop and open up a garage and repair shop. That's only one of his dreams, and he's always telling us not to be afraid to have all the big dreams we want.

I guess mine is to become a teacher, even though my older brother, Cal, says no public school in California would ever hire a Japanese teacher.

"Well," I said to him once, "you're studying at the university to be an engineer, aren't you?"

Cal shrugged and said, "That doesn't mean anybody's going to hire me. I'll probably end up selling cabbages and potatoes at some produce market just like all the other Japanese guys I know."

I hate it when Cal talks like that, because then I think I'll never get to be a teacher after all. Cal knows a lot more than I do, and I usually believe what he tells me.

When I went out to the lot in back of the barbershop, sure enough, there was Papa working under somebody's car. I could see his two feet sticking out, and I yelled at him, "Hey, Papa, you sure are some barber!"

Right away Papa came sliding out, wiping the sweat from his face with his sleeve and squinting up at me and the sun. Even in his dirty overalls, with grease smudged on his face, I thought Papa was good looking. He and my brother, Cal, have large dark eyes and naturally wavy hair that I covet with all my heart. I guess Cal got all the good things because he was born first. By the time I came along, there were only straight hair, small eyes, and skinny legs to go around.

Papa was surprised to see me. "What're you doing here, Rinko?" he asked. "Need another haircut already?"

"I sure hope not," I said.

Papa only has to trim my hair about once a month now that I let it grow long, but I can hardly wait until I'm old enough to go to a beauty parlor for a real haircut. Mama says I have to wait until I'm sixteen, so I still have five more years to go.

Papa was ready to slide back under the car again, so I waved the letter at him and told him about the mess Mama had left in the kitchen. That caught his attention, because he knows Mama would never waste even one drop of water by leaving the faucet dripping. She is so careful, she saves everything from scraps of cloth to pieces of string. She even has a ball of silk thread made of all the tiny pieces of leftover sewing thread tied end to end.

I sat on the ground next to Papa while he read the letter, and he told me it was from Aunt Waka, Mama's sister, who lives in Tokyo. He went through the first few pages fast, because Aunt Waka always wrote about the weather and asked how everybody was and told us about Grandpa and Grandma before she got down to writing about herself.

9

Finally when Papa got to the fourth page, he said, "Well, what do you know, Rinko. Your Aunt Waka is coming to visit us this summer. In fact, she'll be here by the fifteenth of June."

I was really surprised when I heard that, because I never in the world thought I'd ever see Aunt Waka here in America. I always thought of her as Mama's tragic younger sister because of all the misfortunes in her life. First her little boy died of dysentery when he was two, and then her husband died of tuberculosis the year after. So she was living with Grandpa and Grandma, doing some sewing to earn money and helping Grandpa at his pharmacy. I never thought she'd be able to save up enough money to sail across the Pacific Ocean even if she came third class on a Japanese ship. But I guess Mama had sent her a little money to help out.

To tell the truth, I wasn't all that thrilled at the thought of Aunt Waka coming for the whole summer. I knew I'd probably have to give her my room and move in with Joji. I'd have Cal's bed since he was going to Stockton for the summer to pick fruit and earn tuition money for the fall semester. It would be bad enough with Cal gone all summer, I thought, but suppose Aunt Waka turned out to be a melancholy figure who did a lot of weeping and gnashing of teeth?

When I looked at Papa, I saw that he wasn't exactly jumping for joy either. He just gave Aunt Waka's letter back to me and slid under the car again without saying anything more.

I thought Papa was probably thinking the same thing I was about my tragic Aunt Waka, but I was wrong. I didn't know it then, but Papa had a problem that was a lot bigger than having Aunt Waka come. And it wasn't until after supper that I found out what it was.

II

◆◆◆◆◆◆◆◆◆◆◆◆◆◆◆◆◆◆◆◆◆◆◆◆

WHEN I GOT BACK FROM PAPA'S SHOP, JOJI
was home, sitting at the kitchen table chewing on a
piece of ice.

"You know you're not supposed to chip ice off the
block," I warned him. "You know what Mama said
about the icebox."

Joji pushed his felt beanie down over his forehead
and reminded me that Mama wouldn't find out if I
kept my mouth shut. Besides, he said, he deserved
the ice because he hadn't done his lessons for Japanese
Language School and old sourpuss had rapped him on
the knuckles with his ruler.

When I heard that, I relented. "OK then," I said.

After all, I figured I could afford to be a little gen-
erous with Joji since I'd been excused from going to
Japanese Language School for the rest of the year.
The reason this great thing happened was because I
was so skinny. The school nurse sent Mama a note

suggesting that I drink two extra glasses of milk every day and cut down on my after-school activities. Of course, Mama told me immediately that I could skip Japanese Language School for a while because she worries about my health.

I couldn't have been more thrilled, because going to Japanese Language School after regular school was just one more thing to make me different from my classmates. Of course, I missed seeing Tami there, and I knew she'd be ahead of me when I went back next year. But, well, you can't have everything.

I watched Joji crunching and chewing on his piece of ice and told him about Aunt Waka.

"Aw, gee," he moaned. "What's she coming for?"

"To see Mama, of course," I said. "After all, she is her only sister."

"Well, where's she gonna sleep?"

When I told him I'd probably have to give her my room, Joji seemed relieved, but before he felt too good about that I informed him I'd probably have to move in with him and his dog Maxwell, who sleeps in a box at the foot of his bed.

"But you'd better give old Maxie a bath before I move in," I told him.

"What for?" Joji wanted to know

"Because he stinks," I said

"He does not."

"He does too."

13

"Does not."

"Does too."

"Doesn't," Joji muttered under his breath.

I didn't pay any attention to Joji for a while. I was busy washing the rice for supper, swishing it around and around in the pan. I rinsed it over and over until the water wasn't milky any more and had turned clear. Then I filled the pan with water up to the first knuckle of my third finger the way Mama told me to. And I put the pan on the stove so the rice would be ready to cook when Mama got home.

Joji had spread his school books all over the kitchen table right on top of the mess Mama had left and had his nose stuck in one of his books.

"I'm going out to get the eggs now," I told him. And then just before I let the screen door bang behind me, I yelled, "*Does*, Joji. Maxwell does so stink!"

And I ran out before he could answer back. I'm pretty good at getting Joji's goat. I love to tease him because Cal's always doing it to me. Poor old Joji, I guess sometimes he gets it from both Cal and me, and that's probably why he has a dog.

Two years ago he adopted this forlorn-looking bassett hound that followed him home from school one day. He named him Maxwell after his shop teacher, Mr. Maxwell Thornbury, and took him just about every place he ever went. Once he even tried to put him up front near the handlebars of his bike and ride with his arms around him. It was the most comical sight I ever saw.

Personally, I thought Maxwell was just about the homeliest dog I'd ever seen in my entire life. He looked like a little old man draped in a piece of brown velvet that was too long, with the leftover cloth hanging in thick folds under his chin. Not only that, his long droopy ears dragged on the ground, he had sad wet eyes and huge thick paws with splayed toes. I mean, who could love a dog like that, except my brother Joji, aged nine, who is a bit on the homely side himself.

Joji is growing sideways instead of up. And like me, he also missed out on the wavy hair and large eyes. But he's not skinny like I am. He is definitely on the plump side. That's because he loves to eat. He eats almost as much rice as Papa, who often has four bowls of rice for supper. And whenever Joji earns some pennies or a nickel for running errands for our neighbor, Mrs. Sugarman (I call her Mrs. Sugar), he spends it on penny candy instead of putting it in his "going to college" jar like he's supposed to.

His jar has more air in it than money. But mine, I'm happy to say, is almost half full. The trouble is I hardly ever have a chance to earn any money. I can't get a real honest-to-goodness job like Cal, and Mrs. Sugar says she wouldn't send a young lady like me on errands to the corner store. So mostly I get my money for helping Mama or on birthdays.

I told Mrs. Sugar I wouldn't mind doing errands, but she said no, she'd have Joji go to the store for her, and she'd like for me to sit and have tea or cocoa and conversation with her. Well, that's OK too, because I could eat Mrs. Sugar's spice cake and ginger cookies all day long. And besides, she is a kindred soul I can really talk to. Still, I wish I could run an errand for her once in a while.

Anyway, I felt good about getting the last word with Joji that afternoon and went out to confront the chickens in their yard out in back. It's my job every day to collect their eggs from the nests Papa made for them out of old apple boxes. But to tell the honest truth, I've never liked those chickens. I have this awful feeling that one day they're going to pounce on me with their sharp claws and peck me to death for coming every day to take their eggs away from them. I especially try to avoid that mean old rooster who glares at me with his black beady eyes.

A long time ago when I was little, Cal told me I could become invisible if I held my breath. So the entire time I was in the chicken yard, I used to try to hold my breath and practically exploded by the time I came staggering out with the eggs. Of course, I no longer believe I can become invisible, but I still hold my breath anyway when I'm in the chicken yard. I guess it's just a habit I'll always have, like peeling my hangnails until they bleed.

Mama, on the other hand, loves those old hens and talks to them like they were her friends. She thanks them for laying their eggs and tells them she'd never be able to bake her sponge cakes without them.

Mama also talks to the flowers and vegetables she's got planted in the back yard. If anybody who didn't know Mama ever heard her jabbering to herself in the backyard, I suppose they'd think she wasn't quite right in the head. But it's not that. It's just that Mama is an extremely friendly soul and talks to just about anybody or anything.

By the time I came inside with the eggs that day, Mama was home and was already in the kitchen wearing her apron. Usually the first thing she asks when she sees me is, "How was school today?" But that day the first thing she said was, "What do you think, Rinko? Your Aunt Waka is coming to visit us this summer."

"I know," I said. I guess I spoiled her surprise, so I explained how I couldn't wait and had gone to have Papa read the letter to me.

Mama didn't seem to mind that I already knew. She was ecstatic about her sister's coming. After all, Aunt Waka was her only sister and Mama hadn't seen her since the day she sailed for America over twenty years ago to come marry Papa.

I've always wondered how Mama could do such a

17

thing. I mean, leave behind her entire family and sail to a foreign country to marry a man she'd never seen before. I know I'd never do a thing like that. But Mama said that's what a lot of Japanese women did in those days.

"We had faith in our go-betweens who arranged good marriages for us," she told me. "And it all worked out, didn't it?"

I guess it did all right, because here we all are in Berkeley, California—Mama, Papa, my two brothers, and me.

Mama was already talking about all the things we'd do when Aunt Waka got here and the places she'd like to show her. Then she said, "You won't mind giving her your room, will you, Rinko? You can move in with Joji as soon as Cal leaves for Stockton."

"I guess not," I said, not sounding wildly enthusiastic, "as long as Joji gives Maxwell a good scrubbing."

Mama ignored my last remark and went right on talking as though everything was all settled. So I went to look at the back bedroom to see if I could stand being in there with Joji and Maxwell for the whole summer.

The sun was streaming in from the two windows that looked out on Mama's petunias and dahlias, and I could see her string bean vines just beginning to climb up their poles. I decided then that it might not be such a bad place to spend the summer.

My own bedroom is in the middle of the house, between Cal and Joji's room in back and Mama and Papa's room in front. There are doors to each of their rooms, and there's also a door leading to a small hall where the bathroom is. So my room has three doors and everybody is always tramping through my room to get from one place to another.

Also, my room is rather dismal because it has only one window that looks out on the peeling paint on the side of Mrs. Sugar's house. But when I shut all the doors and sit at my desk by the window, it's sort of like being in a dark cave and I feel secure and safe.

I have three "do not disturb" signs to hang on my door knobs for times when I want to be left alone to read or write in my notebook or just think about life in general. Then even Joji knows better than to disturb me. He'll go around through the sun porch to get to wherever he's going, which Cal often does anyway. And Mama and Papa will use their other door that leads into the parlor. But actually, I don't hang up my signs very often. I usually leave all the doors to my room open, because I can be a very accommodating person when I want to be.

I'd decided to see how Cal's bed felt since I'd be sleeping in it all summer. Just as I was bouncing up and down on it and listening to the springs squeak, Cal came walking into the room.

I wasn't expecting him home so early because he usually stayed at the university to study until almost suppertime. He said he couldn't concentrate at home with me and Joji hanging around, but I knew that wasn't the real reason. I knew he stayed to study with his girl friend, Kiyo, who lived in Stockton. And naturally, that was one of the reasons he was going there to work for the summer, although he'd never admit that.

"Hey, what're you doing on my bed, Rink?" Cal asked, sounding not too friendly.

I didn't budge, but I did stop bouncing. "I'm just trying it out," I told him, "since I'll be sleeping here when Aunt Waka comes."

"Yeah, I heard," Cal said. "But she's not here yet, so get moving."

I know when to do as Cal says, so I slid off the bed. When I was out of reach, I said, "OK, California, I'm off your bed."

"What'd you call me, Rink?" He had a definitely menacing look on his face.

"I called you California, your real, honest, and true name, given to you by Uncle Kanda to commemorate your birth in this glorious state," I said.

"OK, Rink, you asked for it."

And just as Cal came lunging at me, I ran screaming toward the sun porch.

"Just be glad you weren't born in Minnesota," I

shouted over my shoulders, "or we'd be calling you Minnie-ha-ha!"

If I hadn't run right into Papa as he came in the back door, I know Cal would have grabbed me and given me what for. Fortunately Papa stepped between us and said calmly, "Why don't you try to behave as though one of you were older?"

That put Cal in his place immediately, and I told Papa he'd just saved my life. But Papa didn't seem to hear me. And he didn't even answer when Mama called out to him.

"What's wrong, Papa?" I asked him.

Papa didn't answer. He just looked distracted. And that's when I knew something was definitely bothering Papa.

III

* *

I CLEARED OFF ALL THE JUNK FROM THE kitchen table and was setting it for supper when I saw Mama sprinkle some curry powder into the stew. That meant there wasn't quite enough stew to go around, and Mama was spicing it up so a little would go further over a big mound of rice.

When the spicy yellow smell began drifting through the house, Mama rang her small black bell. That meant supper was ready. Mama doesn't like calling to us when we're all scattered outside, so she stands at the back door and rings her bell till we come in for supper. I can't always hear the bell when I'm next door, but Mrs. Sugar can hear better than a bird dog and stops in the middle of anything she's saying or doing and hurries me home so I won't be late.

That night everybody happened to be inside, so Mama only had to ring her bell a few times to get us all to the table. Ever since Papa had walked in the back door, Mama'd been talking to him as though she hadn't seen him for a whole week. I saw Papa nodding as Mama went on and on about Aunt Waka's coming.

He washed his hands at the sink and wiped them on the roller towel by the stove, not bothering to roll it around till he'd found a clean spot like I always do. Papa was pretending to listen, but I could tell his mind was a million miles away. I knew exactly what he was doing, because I do that too sometimes. That is, pretend to listen when I'm actually thinking about a dozen other things. Anybody could see Papa was preoccupied, but Mama was too excited to notice.

As soon as we all sat down, Mama said she wanted to say the grace that night instead of Papa.

"Keep it short, Ma," Cal said.

"Yeah, I'm starving," Joji said.

We all knew about Mama's long conversations with God. Every night she sits on her bed with her legs folded underneath, Japanese style, and talks to God as though He lived next door. Some nights she has so much to say to Him, I can hear her mumbling on and on through the walls of my room until I fall asleep.

She began one of her long conversations that night at supper, telling God how grateful she was that her sister was coming at last to visit us and asking Him to watch over Waka as she sailed across the ocean to America. She sounded as though she'd go on for a half hour, but when she stopped for a minute to catch her breath, Papa jumped in and said in a loud voice, "And we thank you for this food. Amen."

We all said amen real fast too, so God would know the rest of us were finished, even if Mama wasn't. I looked up at Papa, expecting him to grin and give me a quick wink. But he was looking down at his plate, pushing his fork into his rice mountain and making the curry run down its sides and puddle up around the edge of his plate. Cal and Joji already had their mouths full.

Mama finally noticed that something was bothering Papa. If she hadn't been so excited about Aunt Waka, she would have known it the minute he got home. Usually she can tell almost immediately when something is wrong with any one of us even if it's only an ingrown toenail, which I often get. Mama says it's because I don't cut my toenails straight across. But I think it's because all the afflictions of my body seem to concentrate in my lower extremities. I also get knee aches which Mama calls "growing pains." Whenever I get those, she gives me some tiny gold seedlike pills that come in a small brown bottle from Grandpa's pharmacy in Tokyo. And if they don't help, she gives me a hot water bottle to take to bed.

"What's wrong, Papa?" she finally asked, when she realized Papa wasn't his usual cheerful self. "No customers today?"

"I didn't want to spoil your good news," Papa

said. "But things are a lot worse than that."

"You behind on the rent again, Pa?" Cal asked.

"More than five months," Papa admitted.

Then he told us the owner had informed him he'd either have to keep up with the rent payments or be evicted. Papa also said his electricity and water would be turned off soon too, if he didn't pay his bills.

"Why don't you borrow money again from the *Tanomoshi?*" I asked Papa. That's the Mutual Finance Association the Japanese people organized to help each other. Everybody puts in some money each month, and then they can borrow from the fund when they need money since none of the banks will give them loans. That was how Papa got started with his barbershop business.

But Papa said he didn't want to borrow from them because he hadn't been able to put in his share lately. "Everybody's having a hard time these days," he said. "Money is just hard to come by."

By then we all felt pretty bad, and even Joji had stopped eating.

"What'll we do if you have to close up your shop?" he asked Papa.

But Papa told us not to worry. "I'll think of something," he said.

I just hoped he wouldn't get any more crazy ideas like the time he wanted to start a chicken farm out in Hayward. I nearly died at the thought of having to collect eggs from several hundred chickens. I certainly couldn't hold my breath *that* long.

There was another time when he wanted to start a restaurant. He said he'd be the cook, Mama and I could wait on tables, and Cal and Joji could wash the dishes. *Nobody* liked that idea. Besides I wasn't so sure anybody would pay good money to eat anything Papa cooked. He just thought he was a good cook because that's what he was when he and Mama first got married and worked for a white family in Oakland.

They took that job so Papa wouldn't have to take Mama down to the farm in the San Joaquin Valley where Papa worked in the potato and onion fields. He said he didn't want Mama to have to work in those hot dusty fields with him and cook for the field hands besides. So she did the washing and cleaning for this white family in Oakland, while Papa tried to cook for them. But Mama said he burned more biscuits and scorched more pans than she cared to remember. Even so, Papa still thinks he's a good cook.

It was terribly depressing to hear Papa talk about all his unpaid bills, and when I looked at him sitting there, looking tired and worried, I noticed he even had a few gray hairs sprouting at his temples.

That was when Cal said, "I could send home the money I earn this summer."

But Mama and Papa said almost simultaneously

that he was to do no such thing and that anything he earned was to be used for his tuition and expenses at the university in the fall.

"Nothing must come before your education," Papa said to Cal. "Not my shop or the rent or anything else. And don't ever forget that."

Cal started to argue back. I thought sure he'd start talking about how a college education wasn't going to do him much good anyway. His mouth was half open, and then he seemed to think better of it and kept quiet.

Thank goodness, I thought. It certainly was no time to have a big argument with Papa. He can get pretty mad when he loses his temper.

Mama brought out a bowl of cabbage she'd pickled with salt and raisins and pressed down with a heavy round stone. She gave Papa his ivory chopsticks—we each have our own special pair, mine is speckled red lacquer—and served him some plain rice in a bowl. Papa poured hot tea over his rice and ate it in a few quick gulps with some pickled cabbage. Then he filled his bowl with hot tea and drank it slowly.

No matter what Mama makes for supper—even chicken dumplings—Papa always has to end his meal with rice, tea and pickles. And he always seems to feel better after he's eaten that. I guess he likes it even better than dessert, because Papa isn't wild about sweets the way Joji and I are. The two of us could eat cake and candy all day long, but for some strange reason, it's only Joji who gets fat.

Well, when Papa finished his rice and pickles and leaned back in his chair, Mama said she had something she wanted to say.

"You know, Mrs. Phillips and her friends often ask if I know someone who could do their wash for them," she began. "In fact, Mrs. Phillips asked me again today if I couldn't come in on Mondays as well as Tuesdays and do her washing and ironing for her."

Papa ran a finger across his mustache. "Do you want to do that?" he asked.

But Mama said, "No, I just had an even better idea. How would it be if I stopped working for Mrs. Phillips altogether and started a home laundry in our basement? I know Mrs. Phillips and her friends would give us their business, and I could make more money than I do now just working for one family."

We were all flabbergasted. I mean, it was Papa who usually had the crazy ideas about a new business, not Mama. We all stared at her to see if she was joking. But she was sitting there straight and stiff, looking very determined, and we could see she meant what she said.

Papa rubbed the back of his neck the way he does when he doesn't know what to say. "Running a home laundry would be hard work, Mama," he said finally. "Are you sure you could manage?"

Mama looked Papa straight in the eye and said, "You know I've never been afraid of hard work. All I need are soap, hot water, and a strong back, and I have all three. Besides," she added, "when Waka comes, I'm sure she'd be willing to help me."

I saw I had a chance to help too, so I said, "Maybe I could iron the flat easy stuff, like the pillow cases and the handkerchiefs." After all, I was already doing that with our own wash, so I figured I could do it for Mama's home laundry as well.

Mama gave me one of her quick smiles that crinkle up her face and said she'd certainly appreciate any help she could get. So Joji offered to help too, although I couldn't imagine what he could possibly do besides get in the way.

By that time, Papa was getting enthusiastic about the idea as well.

"I could look around for an old washing machine to fix up for you," he said to Mama, "and Joji and I could pick up and deliver the laundry."

"In your old Model T?" Cal asked. Papa had bought it third or fourth hand for only $30 and fixed it up like new.

"Why not?" Papa said. "We could hang a sign over the side of the car. It could say, 'Tsujimura A-1 Home Laundry' with our address and phone number on it."

Cal was grinning. "Well, Ma," he said, "looks like

you got yourself a home laundry." And he gave her a little pat on the back before he went off to go study for some exams.

I got up from the table too, because I had a sudden urge to go next door and tell Mrs. Sugar about Mama's new business.

"What about the dishes, Rinko?" Mama asked.

But I was already halfway to the back door. "They'll keep, Mama," I shouted, and I ran toward the hole in the hedge to get to Mrs. Sugar's back yard.

IV

MRS. SUGAR USUALLY LEAVES HER BACK DOOR unlatched, so I just knocked and walked right in. I found her standing at the kitchen sink washing her supper dishes and talking to her pet canary, Lydia.

Mrs. Sugar is a very large person and has the nicest soft lap to sit in. I discovered that when I was a lot younger and used to need comforting on the days when I came home and found Mama out at work. Mrs. Sugar's face looks like a scrubbed red apple because she spends a lot of time in the sun working in her garden, and she has short brown hair that's held back with two curved amber combs.

"Guess what, Mrs. Sugar," I said the minute I walked into her kitchen. "Mama's starting a home laundry."

"She's what?" she asked.

I said hello to her canary, Lydia, and then I told her again about the laundry. I also remembered there

31

was more news, and I told her Aunt Waka was coming to visit us from Japan.

Mrs. Sugar seemed to like the second news best. "Glory be, your Mama must be happy," she said. And she took her soapy hands out of the dishwater and gave me a damp kiss on the cheek.

"But a home laundry," she said. "That sounds like a lot of work for your mama. Doesn't she have enough to do?"

Mrs. Sugar wiped her hands on her apron and just left the rest of her dishes in the sink as though they'd finish washing themselves. Then she took me to the dining room, told me to sit at her round table with its lacy cloth and opened her cupboard to see what she had to give me. She found a tin of English tea biscuits and put some on a plate for me.

"Papa's going to see if he can't find an old washing machine to fix up for Mama," I said. I also told her I was going to help with the ironing.

Mrs. Sugar was just about to bite into a tea biscuit when she suddenly stopped like a toy that's come unwound.

"Well, Rinko," she said, looking enormously pleased with herself. "You just tell your papa his search is ended. I have an old broken-down washing machine sitting right in my basement."

She said she'd been waiting for Mr. Sugarman to fix it for her one day, but he died of pneumonia before he ever got around to it. I think Mr. Sugarman was a nice person, although I don't remember him very well. I know he was a mailman, and the reason he got pneumonia and died was because he kept on delivering the mail in the cold rain one winter when he was sick and should have stayed home in bed.

"Papa could've fixed your washing machine for you," I told her.

But Mrs. Sugar said she was so used to washing everything by hand, she'd even forgotten she had a washing machine.

"After all," she said, "how much laundry is there for just one person? Your mama's welcome to it."

Mrs. Sugar put her biscuit down on the table and insisted we go down that very minute to her basement to look at the machine. I followed her to a dark musty corner and sure enough, there was an old washing machine with a wringer on it. It was half tipped over, like it was drunk, and it looked as though rust had crept into all its joints. I wasn't sure if even Papa could get it to go again.

But Mrs. Sugar said, "You know your papa can fix anything. You tell him and your brother, Cal, to come and get it any time they want."

So the very next day Papa and Cal went over and brought the washing machine back to our basement. Mama and Joji and I watched while they propped it up with a box and set it by the laundry tubs. I could tell Mama thought the same thing I did when I first saw it.

"Do you think you can get it to work?" she asked.

Papa checked the machine carefully and finally said he thought he could.

"It needs a leg, some new hoses, a handle for the wringer and a few other things. But just give me a few days," he said. "I think I can bring it back to life."

"So are we in business then?" Joji asked.

"I guess we are," Mama said.

And that's how we got started with our A-1 Home Laundry.

We all pitched in with cleaning up the basement, which was almost as moldy and cluttered as Mrs. Sugar's. Papa built a counter for sorting and separating the laundry into colored and white, starch and no-starch, and marking everything with indelible ink. He also built a chute by the window so he could just throw the laundry bundles down from his car and they'd land in a big basket right near the washtubs.

Cal rigged up some new clothes lines out in the backyard and also strung up some rope in the basement for days when the wash couldn't be hung outdoors. Our basement looked like some giant spider had gone crazy and spun webs of rope all over the basement beams. Cal was so tall, he had to duck to keep from hanging himself on the ropes, because he'd put them up at the right height for Mama and me to reach.

One afternoon when Mama and I were down in the basement trying to get rid of some empty cartons and old newspapers, Mama came across the big trunk she'd brought with her from Japan. I'd never seen her open it up, so I asked if there was anything inside.

"Oh, yes," Mama said. "My Japanese self."

I didn't know what Mama meant until she blew off the dust on top and lifted the heavy lid of the trunk. The top tray was full of old photograph albums and bundles of letters and Japanese books and notebooks that Mama had used in school. Mama said she'd brought everything in the world she'd owned when she came to America to marry Papa.

She showed me her school notebooks filled with feathery writing in faded dust-colored ink. And she showed me lots of photographs. One was of her family. There were Grandpa and Grandma looking younger than I'd ever seen them, my two uncles wearing school uniforms, and Mama and Aunt Waka when they were twelve and thirteen. Aunt Waka was standing with a crutch, and Mama told me she'd had to use a crutch for a long time because she was born with a deformed foot. But Aunt Waka didn't look sad about it. In fact, she was the only one in the photo who was smiling. Everybody else looked so solemn, they almost seemed sad. But Mama said picture-taking was serious business in those days.

Mama showed me some more photographs, and there was one with rows of young Japanese girls standing in kimonos, their hair piled up on their heads in enormous pompadours. They looked solemn too, and each one was clutching a rolled up diploma.

Mama told me that was her graduation picture from Girls School and asked if I could pick her out. I didn't think I could. But finally, in the very last row, I saw this skinny girl with Mama's eyes.

"Is that you, Mama?"

I couldn't believe it when Mama said I'd found her.

She squinted at the old photograph and began to smile. "Do you know I wanted to become a school teacher then?" she asked.

I was surprised. I'd never before imagined Mama wanting to be anything else than exactly what she was now. It never occurred to me she might have had another kind of dream for herself.

"But if you'd become a teacher," I said, "you might not have come to America to marry Papa."

"That's right," she answered. "So you see, it all worked out for the best, didn't it?"

Mama got very quiet then, and she put everything back in the tray, giving each album a little pat as she put it down. Then she closed the lid and gave that a few pats too, as though she was saying good-bye to everything inside.

"What's in the rest of the trunk?" I really wanted to see more.

"Oh, just my silk kimonos and brocade *obis* and things I don't need any more," Mama said. And she brushed the dust from her hands and went back upstairs to start supper.

I stayed in the basement for a while though, because I had a lot of thoughts muddling around in my head. I felt as if Mama wasn't just plain Mama any more. It was as if part of her was locked up in her big trunk, never able to get out.

It gave me an odd unsettled feeling, like having a pebble in my shoe. I got to wondering if maybe the reason Mama wanted so much for me to be a teacher was because she didn't get to be one herself.

I thought about the smiling girl with the crutch in the photograph, and then I began to feel this terrific curiosity to see what my Aunt Waka would be like. I also wondered if she still had a deformed foot.

Suddenly, I wanted her to hurry up and come, and I ran upstairs to clean out some of the junk in my closet, as though getting ready for her would make her get here sooner.

V

❖◆❖◆❖◆❖◆❖◆❖◆❖◆❖◆❖◆❖◆❖◆❖◆◆

CAL HAD TO LEAVE FOR STOCKTON THE WEEK
before Aunt Waka came, so Mama made him promise
he'd come home one weekend to meet her. Anybody
would have thought Cal was going off to another country the way everyone gave him last minute advice.

"Picking fruit all day won't be easy," Papa warned
him.

And Papa knew what he was talking about. He'd
spent a lot of long hot summers doing it himself when
he first came to America.

"But stick with it, Cal. Work hard and don't get
discouraged," he told him.

"Be careful not to fall off those tall ladders," Mama
said. "Eat plenty, and don't fritter away all your
money."

"All what money?" Cal asked.

He was going to earn $12\frac{1}{2}$¢ an hour picking pears
for ten hours every day and his board and room was

38

going to cost him 50¢ a day.

I knew Cal would be busy with a lot more than just picking fruit what with his girl friend in the same town. So I reminded him not to forget to write. And he reminded me not to mess around with his things.

"You too, Joj," he said, and he gave him a poke in the ribs, which Joji immediately tried to return.

Until then I was sort of anxious for Cal to leave so I could move into his room. But when I saw him heave his duffel bag on his shoulder and say, "Well, so long everybody," I almost began to cry.

Joji and I fight a lot, but there's something special between Cal and me. Almost anything he does is OK by me, and I was already beginning to ache with missing him.

I wanted to give him a hug, but I knew he'd be embarrassed if I did. We don't hug or kiss much in our family. That doesn't mean we don't love each other, because of course we do.

Mrs. Sugar says it's probably because of the way Mama and Papa grew up in Japan. "I believe people only bow to each other in Japan," she explained. "They don't do a lot of hugging like I do. But that's fine too. There are lots of other ways to show you care about somebody."

I guess that's what I was doing, because I gave Cal a punch on the arm instead and told him to bring me some pears when he came home.

Cal punched me back, but not too hard, and said, "I might, if you behave yourself." And then he was gone.

I felt so lonesome, I right away picked a fight with Joji. I told him I was planning to move my stuff into his room right then and for him to go wash his dog immediately.

Joji just glared at me and pushed his beanie down on his forehead. "I'll do it when I'm good and ready," he said. "And that might be never!"

"Well, you know what you are, Joji?" I answered. "You are just impossible, that's what."

And I huffed past him to go phone Tami. Maybe she could come over, I thought, and fill up the empty space Cal had left in the house.

Our telephone is in the narrow hallway between the kitchen and the bathroom and my bedroom. It's practically impossible to have any privacy there. But I closed all the doors and didn't bother to turn on the light. I sat there in the dark and picked up the receiver and waited for the operator to come on the line. In a minute she was there saying, "Number, please," sounding like she was holding her nose.

I knew Tami's number by heart, of course.

"Berkeley 7646W," I said good and loud, speaking up so the operator would get it right the first time and I could say "Yes, please," without having to repeat it.

My teacher at school is always asking me to repeat my answers.

"Rinko, you'll have to learn to speak up," she says, as though having a soft voice was a fault I'd have to overcome.

I don't know why I can't speak up in class. I certainly can make myself heard when I'm at home. And when I'm having conversations with people inside my head, I'm always speaking up, telling them exactly what I think in a loud, firm voice.

But at school it's different. If you feel like a big nothing and don't like who you are, naturally you don't speak up in a loud, firm voice. You don't talk to other people either, unless they talk to you first.

At school I feel sort of pressed down and small and not my own real true self. And I guess maybe that's why I slouch a lot. Mama is always telling me to straighten up and stand up tall.

"You're looking like a cat again, Rinko," she says.

But Mama doesn't really know why I always slouch. And I can't seem to tell her or Papa. In fact, I can't talk to anybody about the way I feel at school. Not to Cal or to my best friend, Tami, or to Mrs. Sugar.

All the time I was sitting in the dark hallway listening to Tami's phone ringing, I was hoping her mother wouldn't answer the phone.

Actually Tami's mother isn't one of my favorite people. She has bulging eyes, which Mama says are

41

caused by a thyroid condition, and she is always trying to run everybody else's life. In fact, she spends a lot of time trying to find suitable wives for the bachelors from Japan who live in the dormitory in back of our Japanese church.

Sometimes I think all her mama's talk is rubbing off on Tami, because she talks about getting married herself. And that's stupid. She's barely twelve and certainly doesn't have to start looking for a husband yet.

When I told Tami that Aunt Waka was coming and mentioned that she was a widow, the first thing she said was, "Oh, in that case, maybe Mama can find a nice husband for her."

"How about Uncle Kanda?" I asked.

Of course, I was only kidding. Who would ever want to marry Uncle Kanda? Once when Mama didn't know I was listening, I heard her say he likes money more than anything else. And Tami's mother said he was a miser who would walk ten miles to save spending a nickel for streetcar fare. She also said she heard he kept all his money in a money belt wound around his waist and that he even wore it to bed every night.

Besides, Uncle Kanda was too old for anybody to marry, although Papa did say he wasn't as old as he looks. He said Uncle Kanda's hair turned white overnight when the lady he was supposed to marry jumped out of a window and killed herself two days after she arrived from Japan.

"Did she do that because she didn't want to marry Uncle Kanda after she came to America and saw him?" I asked.

Papa didn't answer yes or no. He just said, "That would be a terrible thought to live with, wouldn't it?"

I guess that's why Uncle Kanda never got married and still lives all alone in that musty room above his dry cleaners.

Tami is so crazy she actually believed her mother could fix up Aunt Waka with Uncle Kanda. "I'll tell her to try," she said, as though I'd been serious when I suggested him.

Well, Tami did answer the phone that day I called, but it turned out she couldn't come over because she had to help her mother clean house. She told me, however, that she'd be coming next Saturday when Aunt Waka arrived.

"Mama's going to make some vinegared rice balls with fresh tuna, and we're coming over to welcome your auntie," she told me.

"Swell," I said, although I wished her mother would bring some cream puffs oozing with whipped cream instead.

Tami said her mama could hardly wait to meet Aunt

Waka to see if she'd be suitable for Uncle Kanda. And pretty soon, I began to wonder myself if maybe it might really work out.

Papa killed two chickens for Aunt Waka's welcome dinner. The minute I heard the squawking out in the chicken yard, I covered my ears and ran inside. I can't bear to hear the racket whenever Papa goes out to catch a chicken, and I hate the smell when he singes off the pinfeathers over an open fire. I stay out of the backyard until I'm sure Papa is all finished with everything because I can't stand seeing those headless corpses with their bloody dangling necks.

But when Mama cuts up the chicken meat and cooks it in soy sauce with sugar and ginger, it smells so good I forget about the gory mess and can't wait to get some in my mouth. I sometimes wonder if maybe there's a little bit of cannibal in me.

The morning Aunt Waka's ship was to dock in San Francisco, Mama was up and fussing from 6 o'clock in the morning. Not only that, she'd spent the entire week before washing the curtains and cleaning the house, and I helped her polish all the furniture and mop the floors. It was just like New Year's, when Mama says we have to begin the new year with a clean house as well as clean hearts and spirits. You would have thought the Empress of Japan herself was coming, not just Mama's sister.

44

Mama also spent several days preparing the kind of food she makes for New Year's. She cooked bamboo shoots and burdock and taro and lotus root, and knots of seaweed and sweet black beans and herring roe (which I don't like), and shredded long white radish with sesame seed. She put everything in tiered lacquer boxes and set them out in the cooler. The morning we were going to meet Aunt Waka, she cooked a big pot of rice and wrapped it up in the quilt on her bed to keep warm until we got back.

All the time Mama was fixing the food, she had a worried look on her face. Finally she said, "My, I do hope Waka will be able to eat all this when she gets here."

"Why wouldn't she?" I asked.

I hoped Aunt Waka wasn't going to be a pale and finicky eater as well as a tragic presence. That would be a terrible bore, I thought, because I love to eat myself.

But Mama said she was just remembering how she'd felt herself the day she arrived from Japan.

"I was wobbly and weak from being seasick for two whole weeks, and my clothes reeked of the fish they cooked every day in the ship's galley," she explained. "I couldn't eat for days after I arrived."

Then she told me how awful it had been at the Immigration Station on Angel Island where she and most of the other people on the ship had to wait until they were examined to make sure they didn't have hook-worm or trachoma or tuberculosis.

"Then did they let you go?"

"Yes, finally, after four days." Mama looked miserable just remembering. "But all that time I didn't know whether I'd be able to stay in America. And your poor Papa was waiting for me in San Francisco, not knowing whether he'd have a bride or not.

Mama told me how she used to lie in her narrow bunk in that dormitory full of strangers on Angel Island and cry every night because she was so homesick.

"Did you wish you'd never come?" I asked her.

"Oh, many times, Rinko."

After a few minutes Mama wiped her forehead, like she was wiping away the sadness.

"Well, thank goodness your Aunt Waka won't have to go through all that," she said. "They don't hold people at Angel Island anymore and besides, the ships are bigger now, so she probably didn't even get seasick."

"Then she'll be able to eat, probably."

Mama smiled at me. "I'm sure of it," she said, and she asked me to help her set the dining room table with her good china.

I guess Papa thought Aunt Waka was more important than his barbershop, because he closed it up even if it was a Saturday so we could all go meet her at the pier. "It isn't every day that Waka comes from Japan," he said.

Papa and Joji were out in the car long before Mama even put on her hat. I heard Papa prime the motor and crank it up, all ready to go. But Mama had certain things she had to do whenever she went out.

First she checked to make sure the gas on the stove was turned off and the faucets weren't dripping. Then she made sure all the windows were locked and the water pan under the icebox was emptied. Then she reminded me to take down the sign in the window for the iceman so he wouldn't leave any ice that day. And finally, she put on her hat and stuck a big hat pin into her bun to hold it in place.

Mama and I climbed into the back seat, and the four of us finally went rattling off in Papa's Model T, all dressed up in our Sunday clothes and looking like we were going to church.

Papa drove as if somebody was chasing him all the way to the Oakland pier, and Mama kept clutching my arm and calling out to him.

"Slow down, Papa. Do be careful or we will all be killed before we even see Waka."

But Papa just waved at her and said, "Stop worrying, Mama, I'm a very good driver and, besides, we can't be late."

47

It was a good thing Papa drove fast because we were the last car to get on the 11 o'clock ferry for San Francisco. I looked at the clock and thought in just one more hour I would meet Aunt Waka at last.

VI

AUNT WAKA'S SHIP, THE *Taiyo Maru,* WAS AL-
ready docked when we got to Pier 35. I was surprised
at how high it rode in the water, and a long gangplank
was pushed up for the first and second class passengers. There was a shorter one toward the stern for the
people in third class, and that's where we went to wait
for Aunt Waka.

Every time a Japanese lady came down the gangplank, Joji would holler, "There she is! Is that her?"

And Mama would shake her head and say, "No, not
yet, not yet."

After a while Mama got nervous. "Suppose she isn't
on the ship, Papa? Suppose something happened to
her?"

But Papa only said, "For heaven's sake, Mama,
what on earth could happen to her? Where could she
go? Of course she's on the ship."

We waited and waited while a lot more people came

down the gangplank. Then suddenly Mama called out, "There she is! Waka! Waka!"

And before Papa could stop her, Mama pushed her way right past all the people in front of us and climbed halfway up the gangplank to greet her sister.

Aunt Waka was wearing a blue kimono with wavy white stripes rippling down it like a lot of little rivers, and her hair was piled up in a bun on top of her head. I was surprised to see how gray it was, since she's younger than Mama. I thought probably it was because of all the tragedies in her life.

I took a quick look at her feet, but couldn't tell if anything was wrong with either one. She did have a slight limp though, and was having a hard time trying to hold onto the railing with one hand and carry a small cloth bundle in the other.

Mama took the bundle from her, and the two of them came down together, talking like they'd never stop. Aunt Waka bowed at least a half dozen times to Papa, saying all the proper polite things she was supposed to say. And Papa bowed back, but not as many times.

"We're all so glad you've come, Waka," he said to her.

When she got to me, she smiled just the way Mama does, crinkling up her eyes. *"Mah,* Rinko," she said. "How nice to meet you at last."

I didn't know what to say back to her, so I asked if she got seasick, and she said only for the first few days.

"That's good," I said. "Then you can eat all the good stuff Mama made for you."

And thank goodness, she said she certainly could.

Joji didn't know what to say to her either. He just stuck out his hand and shook hers, looking as solemn as a little owl. He didn't utter a sound. He does that sometimes when Mama and Papa's friends are over for Sunday dinner. While we're waiting for Papa to say the grace, he will sit at the dining room table separating all the food on his plate so the rice and the meat and the vegetables don't touch each other. Then he won't say a single word during the entire meal, not even to me. He can be so boring. That's why I like to invite Tami to come over on Sundays so I'll at least have somebody to talk to.

I sat in the back seat of the car with Mama and Aunt Waka, and they talked and laughed and cried all the way home. Mama told her about our new home laundry, but mostly they talked about how things were when they were growing up in Japan.

I watched Aunt Waka out of the corner of my eye, trying not to stare at her. So far she didn't sound like she'd be such a bleak, sorrowful presence, but it was still too early to tell.

51

When we were almost home, Aunt Waka turned to me and asked if I was healthier now, and I told her I was.

"I drink two extra glasses of milk every day," I said, sounding like a five-year-old and feeling like a stupid ninny.

But Aunt Waka just said, "That's good, Rinko. I brought you more medicine for your knee aches too." And she reached out and patted my knees.

I wished Mama hadn't written Aunt Waka every single detail of my life.

"I guess I get those because I'm trying to grow too fast," I explained.

"Like a noodle," Aunt Waka said.

Suddenly we both laughed. And that was when I thought maybe Aunt Waka was going to be an OK person after all.

As soon as we got home, she wanted to open up her big willow basket and give us all the presents she'd brought. So Papa untied the ropes and opened it up, and I sat on the bed and watched her take everything out.

Grandma and Grandpa had sent all kinds of things, like cans of new spring tea and salt rice crackers, packages of dried seaweed and mushrooms, and big chunks of bonita as hard as rocks, for shaving into flakes to make broth. They sent a lot of stuff from the pharmacy too, like the small brown bottles with my tiny gold pills, and packages of herbs for curing colds and stomach disorders, and plasters for back and shoulder aches.

There were presents for each of us from Aunt Waka too. She brought silk neckties for Papa and Cal, a handwoven shawl for Mama, a set of water colors for Joji, and for me, a silk kimono she'd sewn herself.

"Try it on, Rinko," she said, when she gave it to me.

"I'll do it later on," I said.

What I really had in mind was that I'd put it in Mama's trunk in the basement with all her kimonos and probably never look at it again. Actually, I wished she'd brought me something I could make use of, like Joji's water colors. But I tried not to look too envious.

Mama put all the food out on the dining room table, and pretty soon people from church came over with even more food. Mrs. Sugar came too, with a two-layer spice cake, but she didn't stay long because she couldn't understand all the Japanese talk. She surprised Aunt Waka by giving her a big hug, and Aunt Waka surprised her back by speaking some English she'd learned in school. I found out Aunt Waka knew a lot more English than I thought she'd know.

I avoided all the bowing and greeting and jabbering going on in the parlor by staying in the kitchen to fill the teapots with hot water.

The minute Tami came with her mother, she came rushing into the kitchen to look for me. I saw that she had on her good Sunday dress too, and she'd stuck a ribbon in her hair. Tami has long hair that's parted on the side, and whenever it's a special occasion, she ties a big bow in it.

Tami is prettier than I am. She has bigger eyes and very fair skin, which she protects by using her mother's freckle cream. She is also about two inches taller than I am. Like Cal, she got all the good things because she came first. In fact, I guess she got everything there was to get, because she is an only child, which I'm certainly glad I'm not.

I hate to admit it, but Tami is also braver than I am. Like the time when we got turned away at the Crystal Plunge and the lady wouldn't let us in to swim there. I was so embarrassed, I just wanted to run and hide. But Tami just stood there and asked, "Why not? Why can't we go in?"

"Because I know you wouldn't enjoy it here."

"We would too," Tami kept saying.

But the lady gave Tami a funny kind of smile and said, "I'm sorry, I can't sell you a ticket."

By that time everybody else in line was staring at us, and I wanted to disappear into the sidewalk, so I finally pulled Tami away, and we came back home.

The first thing Tami said to me when she came

bursting into the kitchen that afternoon was, "Where's Uncle Kanda?"

"You mean your mama wants to start matching them up already?"

"Why not?" Tami wanted to know. "The sooner the better. If your Aunt Waka gets married here, she won't have to go back to Japan."

"Mama would like that, all right," I said.

Uncle Kanda couldn't come until after he'd closed up his shop, and by that time most of the people had gone home. But Tami and her mama waited for him.

Tami and I watched Papa introduce him to Aunt Waka, and she bowed six times to him, just like she did to Papa. I guess she was showing him respect because of his white hair, not knowing, of course, that he wasn't all that old and decrepit, even though he did look sort of hunched up like a gray dormouse. But that was because he did so much close work and that was why he wore those glasses with the thick lenses.

"Well, why don't we all sit down and have supper?" Papa said, as though we hadn't been eating all afternoon.

So Mama heated up the soybean soup, and we all sat down again to eat with Uncle Kanda so he'd have some company. He said how nice it was to have Sunday dinner with us even if it was only Saturday. And I was afraid he thought he'd already used up his visit for the week, so I told him he could come again the next day like he usually did.

He smiled at me then and said, "Thank you, Rinko. That's a nice thought to hold onto."

Tami's mother sat next to Aunt Waka and told her every good thing she knew about Uncle Kanda, like how he was the best tailor in Berkeley and had a prosperous dry cleaning business near Papa's barbershop and was a pillar of our Japanese church.

I saw Aunt Waka nodding and trying to be polite. But she was also yawning without opening her mouth, which is very hard to do. I know because I do that a lot myself when I have to sit in church and listen to those boring sermons.

Every once in a while Uncle Kanda would lean toward Aunt Waka and ask her a question like, "How was the crossing on the *Taiyo Maru?*" or "Tell me, are your parents quite well?"

Every time Aunt Waka smiled and answered him, Tami would poke me with her elbow or kick my foot or try to wink at me. Sometimes Tami can be so obvious, she is just as bad as her mother. I was sure Aunt Waka must be catching on by then to what they were up to. It was downright embarrassing.

I didn't really have a chance to talk to Aunt Waka myself until we were all getting ready for bed and I smelled incense coming from her room.

"Hey, Joji, do you smell incense?" I asked.

Joji rubbed his nose. "Yeah, it sure stinks."

"Maybe Aunt Waka is trying to purify my room!"

"She's probably trying to get rid of all your germs."

I ignored Joji's remark and tried to peek through the keyhole into what used to be my room. But I couldn't see a thing because I always leave the keys in the keyholes so no one can look in on me. I guess it served me right, not being able to see anything then. But I could hear Aunt Waka mumbling in a low voice, the way Mama does when she's saying her prayers.

By then I was so curious, I couldn't stand it. So I knocked on her door and walked in before Aunt Waka could answer.

"I forgot my bathrobe," I said, fibbing. "It's in my closet."

Aunt Waka was standing at my bureau with her hands clasped, and I saw she'd set up a small Buddhist altar on top of it. There were photographs of her husband and little boy beside it and a stick of incense and a dish with two cookies on it in front of the pictures.

"I was just telling my husband and little boy I'd arrived safely in America," she told me. "I always talk to them when I pray for them."

"Oh."

I felt like I'd barged in on something private and special that I had no business seeing. How strange, I thought, that Aunt Waka was a Buddhist when Mama was such an ardent Christian. What was going to happen, I wondered, when Mama took Aunt Waka to our church and made her sing, "Jesus Savior, Pilot Me," and pray to the God who was her own special friend.

Aunt Waka suddenly seemed like a stranger I might never really get to know. And how were we ever going to take her any place if she went everywhere in a kimono?

I started to back out of the room, but she told me to come in. She didn't seem to mind if I watched her finish with her praying.

"What're the cookies for?" I asked. I knew very well her husband and little boy couldn't come out of the photo to eat them.

Aunt Waka smiled. "It's just a gesture," she said. "It makes me feel as though I've shared something nice with them."

Then she surprised me by giving me one of the cookies and taking the other herself. "You and I will eat them for my little boy," she said. "I think he'd like that."

"But I've already brushed my teeth."

"That's all right. One little cookie won't hurt."

I really wanted to stay and talk with Aunt Waka, but I heard Mama's footsteps coming from the kitchen.

"I'll take it back to bed with me," I said, and I rushed out forgetting all about the bathrobe I was supposed to look for.

Joji and Maxwell were already snoring, but I

pulled the covers over my head so I wouldn't make too much noise crunching my cookie. I could feel the crumbs getting all over my bed and knew they'd probably end up between my toes. But I was busy thinking about Aunt Waka and how different she seemed from Mama. It wasn't just because she'd come from Japan. It was something else. Something that made her seem sort of special. I wasn't sure what it was, but then I had all summer to find out.

VII

IT WAS THE WEEK AFTER AUNT WAKA ARRIVED
that we got the awful threat in the mailbox. Joji was
the one who found it when he went out to make Maxwell stop barking at the mailman.

Maxie was always barking at the wrong people. He
barked at the garbageman, the mailman, the iceman,
and the Japanese peddler who came around in his rat-
tly old truck to sell vegetables and beancurd cakes.

"But they're all *supposed* to come," I told Joji.
"I'll bet if a burglar ever showed up, Maxie wouldn't
even have the sense to bark at him."

"He would too, you just wait and see," Joji said,
sticking up for his dog. "Someday you're gonna find
out what a good watchdog he is."

When Joji picked up the mail that day, he found a
sheet of yellow paper folded up without an envelope.
The minute he read it he came rushing down to the
basement where Mama and I were showing Aunt

Waka how we do the laundry.

Papa had hooked up a heater under the washing machine to keep the water hot through more than one wash, since it takes so long for a tankful of water to heat up. Then Mama and I could rinse the first batch while the second one was washing in the machine.

I hate rinsing things in a tub of cold water. My arms get red clear up to my elbows, and after a while the skin on my fingers puckers up like shriveled prunes. I especially hate rinsing sheets and that huge long cotton underwear that grows enormous when it's wet. Mama and I usually do those together. I do a lot of groaning and moaning because they're so heavy, and sometimes Mama stops and rubs her back.

"Ah, *shindo*," she'll sigh, to let me know she's tired too. Then we both stop and take a little rest.

When Aunt Waka saw us rinsing, she said she was used to hard work and would help Mama in my place while she was here. I thought that was pretty nice of her, especially since she was supposed to be here on a vacation.

"That'll really be peachy-keen," I said. But I don't think she knew what I was talking about.

When Joji came bursting into the basement yelling something about a threat, I thought he was just trying to be funny. But when I read the note myself, I felt sick to my stomach.

It was printed in large black letters and said, "GET

61

OUT OF OUR TERRITORY JAP LAUNDRY, OR YOU'LL BE SORRY."

"Mama," I screamed. "What'll we do?"

At first Mama looked scared too, but then she switched the washing machine back on and said, "We're just going to keep right on working, Rinko."

She told Joji to take the note to Papa at his shop, and she told me to go and hang out the first batch of wash.

Aunt Waka said she'd help me, and she took one handle of the laundry basket full of wet wash while I took the other. We lugged it up the basement steps and out into the backyard together. I guess the chickens thought they were going to get fed, because they came clucking up to their fence, peering at us from between the morning glories Mama had planted there. But I was too worried about the scary note to bother with the chickens.

"Why would anybody want to threaten your mama's laundry?" Aunt Waka asked me. She had a puzzled frown on her face.

"I guess because we're Japanese," I explained. "A lot of people hate us."

"I just don't understand," Aunt Waka said. And she snapped the wet towels real hard to get the wrinkles out and hung them up fast with a fistful of clothespins.

Nobody said anything more about the note all day,

not even Papa when he came home. When I asked him about it, he just said, "It's probably somebody playing a joke on us, Rinko. Don't worry about it."

But Papa was wrong. A few days later, somebody slashed all the tires on his car during the night. It was a good thing he had a lot of spares out in the lot behind his shop. He put those on in a hurry so he and Joji could go pick up laundry bundles that afternoon.

I asked Papa if I could go with him since I knew Aunt Waka was helping Mama.

"I don't see why not," Papa said, "if your chores are done."

They weren't. I hadn't collected the eggs yet, and I still had another roll of damp pillow cases to iron. But I didn't tell Papa. I just went with him.

Joji sat up in front with Papa, and I sat in the back, which I like having all to myself. I watched the houses grow bigger and better as we went up toward the hills, and I envied the view they got from their windows.

Once when Mama went to help Mrs. Phillips cook and serve for a big dinner party, she told us how she could see the entire bay from the kitchen window. She said she watched the sun sink like a red balloon right into the bay, and the sky turned all gold and pink and lavender. And the very next day she had Papa drive us all up to the hills so we could see the sunset for ourselves. Mama was right. It really was beautiful, and I stared hard so the colors would sink into my eyeballs and my head and stay there forever.

We can't see the bay at all from any of our windows. In fact, I doubt if we could even see it from our roof since we're down in the flatlands. The only views we have are of Mrs. Sugar's house on one side and an empty lot full of weeds on the other. And I guess we wouldn't have known what we were missing if Mama hadn't seen that sunset from Mrs. Phillips' kitchen window.

Well, when Papa got to the first house on his pickup list that day, Joji ran out to get the bundle from the front porch. I had a piece of Juicy Fruit gum in my mouth and was counting to see how many times I could chew on it before he got back. But I only got to ten because he came running back empty-handed.

"There's no bundle there," he told Papa. "I rang the bell too, but nobody's home."

"Well, never mind, Joji," Papa said. "Maybe they just forgot."

But when we went to the next house, there was no bundle there either. Or at the house after that. By that time Papa knew something was wrong. When we got to Mrs. Phillips' house, Papa got out himself and rang her doorbell.

I watched him lift his cap and ask Mrs. Phillips if she'd forgotten to put out her bundle.

"Why, no, Mr. Tsujimura," I heard her answer. "I put it out before noon, just as I always do."

Then she came out on the porch and looked all around, even in her rose bushes, as though the bundle might somehow have gotten itself lost among the roses.

She was wearing a green print dress with silk stockings and high-heeled shoes, and she looked like she was going to church or a party, which seemed odd on a Monday. But I guess every day must seem like Sunday to her since she has somebody to do her laundry and ironing and housecleaning for her. Her hair was marcelled in neat, tight waves like she'd just been to the beauty parlor or maybe even waved it herself with a curling iron.

I got to wondering how Mama would look if she marcelled her hair and put rouge on her face like Mrs. Phillips. Mama's hair is straight and black without even a flicker of a wave, and she pulls it back tight into a bun at the back of her neck.

The only thing I've ever seen Mama put on her face is powder from a tiny pink booklet filled with thin pages of powder that Aunt Waka sent her from Japan. Every Sunday morning she tears out a sheet and rubs it over her forehead and nose to take off the shine before she goes to church. Whenever I smell that powder I know it's Sunday, just like I know it's Monday by the smell of the clean starched apron Mama gets out for the week.

I waved at Mrs. Phillips and said hello.

"Hello there, Rinko," she called back. "Tell your

mama I miss her terribly and wish she'd come back and work for me again."

"I'll tell her," I said.

But I really hoped Mama wouldn't go back to work for her. I'd rather have Mama working for herself and her own laundry than doing all that work for somebody else.

Papa and Mrs. Phillips got into a long discussion about the missing bundles, and I heard Papa tell her he thought our bundles had been stolen by somebody who wanted to drive us out of business.

"Why, who on earth would do a thing like that?" Mrs. Phillips asked.

"The Starr Laundry," Papa told her. "But will you stay on with us?"

"Why, of course I will," Mrs. Phillips said.

So Papa asked her not to put her bundle out next week until after the Starr Laundry closed at 5:30 and their trucks stopped running.

"Then I'll come by later on to pick it up," he said.

I wondered how Papa knew it was the Starr Laundry that stole our bundles, and I asked him the minute he cranked up the motor and got back in the car.

Papa didn't want to tell Joji and me. But he said, "Well, I suppose I'll have to tell your mama anyway."

So he told us how one of the Starr trucks had followed him for his entire route the last time he made deliveries.

"Of all the nerve!" I exploded.

"They must've got the addresses of all our customers," Joji said.

Papa nodded. "That's what they did all right, and they picked up all our bundles before we got here. But just wait," he said, "we're going to outsmart them."

And we went back to every house on our route and Papa asked each customer to do the same thing he'd asked Mrs. Phillips.

I guess most of them said they would, because by the time we headed for home I could tell Papa was feeling better. He was singing, *"Kiso no ontaké san"* which he often sings when he's in a good mood.

"Well, I guess we've got the Starr Laundry licked," he said, looking pleased.

But Papa didn't know then how vicious they could get.

VIII

MAMA AND AUNT WAKA HAD JUST HUNG UP A wash and were standing at the hedge talking with Mrs. Sugar when we got back. I thought Mama was probably telling Mrs. Sugar how the new smelly manure was making her petunias and zinnias bloom like crazy.

I could hear the three of them laughing, and I guess if Joji hadn't charged out of the car shouting that our bundles had been stolen, they probably would've gone to Mrs. Sugar's for some tea and spice cake. And I would've been invited too.

When Papa told them what the Starr Laundry had done, Mrs. Sugar bristled like an angry porcupine.

"Why, that's the most underhanded, lowdown thing I've ever heard of," she fumed. "You ought to report them to the police."

Mama kept asking Papa what we should do. "Suppose they come back and do more than slash your tires next time?" she asked.

68

That was when Joji had his brilliant idea.

"Maxie can guard the house," he said, as though that would solve everything. "I'll put him outside at night, and he'll bark at anybody who comes messing around."

That would certainly be better than having both Joji and Maxie snoring in the same room with me, I thought.

What I said was, "I sure hope he barks at the right people for a change."

"He will," Joji said. "You wait and see. He's gonna be the best watchdog you ever saw "

But when it grew dark, Joji didn't want to put Maxie outside. He didn't do it that night or the next night either.

I asked him when he was going to get around to it, but he just said, "Maxie told me he didn't want to sleep outside."

I think my little brother Joji really does believe he and Maxwell can talk to each other.

Well, in the meantime, I wrote a six page letter to Cal and told him about the threat and the slashed tires and the stolen bundles and everything. I guess it was a pretty depressing letter, because I also told him our laundry wasn't doing so well any more either. Some of our customers had changed their minds and were giving their business to the Starr Laundry after all.

In a few days I got a postcard from Cal saying he'd be home the next Saturday. Mama got so excited.

"What time?" she asked, as if I'd know. "Will he be back in time for lunch? For supper?"

"Golly, Mama, I don't know."

So she baked a sponge cake on Friday, and on Saturday she started cooking things right after breakfast.

Aunt Waka worried about where Cal would sleep since she'd taken up one of our beds. I told her Cal could even sleep standing up or in the bathtub if he had to, but he'd probably sleep on the parlor sofa.

Saturday is always housecleaning day at our house. As soon as Papa leaves for the barbershop, Mama sprinkles damp tea leaves all over the floors to keep down the dust while she sweeps.

My job is to dust all the furniture and run the carpet sweeper over the rugs. Joji cleans out the chickenyard, mows the front lawn, and waters the garden.

Usually Mama has to remind me a couple of times that it's Saturday so I'll get started with my dusting. But that was one Saturday I began early so I'd be all through by the time Cal got home. In fact, it was only 10:30 when I'd finished.

Mama had done her cooking and was down in the basement with Aunt Waka doing a wash. I knew I should be picking up my half of the bedroom, but I decided to sit awhile and rest my bones in Papa's big easy chair. The house was really quiet with nobody around except me. So I just leaned back and contemplated the ceiling and wished Cal would hurry home.

I noticed the spot on the ceiling was a lot bigger than when I last looked at it. Every year when the rainy season starts, Papa says he's going to put new shingles on our roof, but he keeps putting it off. And now the spot that looked like a cat last year looks more like a pregnant cow. If Papa doesn't fix the roof pretty soon, that spot will probably spread out over the whole ceiling like a giant dinosaur.

Every once in a while, Mama says she's going to fix up our parlor. She says she's going to make new slipcovers for the chairs and save enough to buy a new rug because this one's unraveling at the edges. But whenever she has any extra money, she puts it in our "going to college" jars, or gives a small donation to the WCTU (that's the Women's Christian Temperance Union in which she's a member), or puts it in the bank for a rainy day. I was thinking her rainy day might come sooner than she thought if the Starr Laundry didn't stop bothering us.

I was squeezing a pimple on my chin with my thumbs while I sat there looking up at the fat cow on the ceiling. I knew I'd have a red swollen chin if I didn't stop, but I was getting jittery waiting for Cal. I also gave myself two new hangnails and went to the bathroom three times.

Finally I heard a car stop and ran to open the front door, and there was Cal coming toward me two steps at a time. He looked tanned and heavier and taller even.

"Hey, you look different," I said.

"I am. I gained six pounds."

Then Cal shoved a big paper sack full of pears at me.

"Here," he said. "I remembered."

The pears smelled wonderful—like summer and the sun and sweet fruity juices. I couldn't wait to eat one, and while I did, leaning over the kitchen sink, Cal went down to the basement to meet Aunt Waka. I heard him calling out to Joji, too, to let him know he was home.

When Papa came home for supper, he brought Uncle Kanda with him, and that was when we really celebrated Cal's homecoming. Uncle Kanda brought over two big bottles of celery phosphate, which I love, and a bottle of saké for himself and Papa.

I think Uncle Kanda was just as happy as Papa to see Cal. He pumped his hand up and down and said, "So, California, you're earning enough money for your college tuition, are you?"

I think Uncle Kanda is the only person who can get away with calling Cal by his real name, since he's the one who gave it to him. Cal didn't say a word about that or answer Uncle Kanda's question, for that matter. He just told Uncle Kanda he was doing fine and to feel the muscles in his arm.

Cal was like the shining star on top of the Christmas tree. He was the special person who made it seem like a holiday, and everybody kept smiling at him and wanting to know all about how he picked fruit and what he did in the evenings and all the rest.

Aunt Waka treated him almost the way she does Papa, because he is the first-born and the eldest son. That counts for a lot in Japan, I guess. She kept saying how happy she was to meet him at last, and she kept his rice bowl filled and poured his tea for him. But she did that for Uncle Kanda too, because when I set the table, I put her ivory chopsticks and her teacup at the place between Cal and Uncle Kanda. I thought Tami and her mama would be real proud of me for thinking to do that.

Everybody was feeling so good, I was really sorry when Cal spoiled everything with his announcement. He didn't even have the sense to wait until after Papa'd had his rice and pickles.

"I'm thinking of dropping out of college and working awhile," he said, as though he was just asking me to pass the pickled cabbage.

Everything came to a complete stop at the table. It was like the times when the machine breaks down at the Japanese movies they show at the Buddhist Temple and everything freezes.

"What?" Papa said at last.

Then Cal talked real fast so he could get everything out before Papa got too excited. He said he wanted to get another job at one of the farms in Stockton after the fruit season ended. He said he wanted to send money home for a while, until things got better.

"I know you're getting hassled," he said, "and I know things are rough for you and Ma right now."

Cal looked down and began talking to his plate.

"Besides," he said in a low voice, "what's the point of getting a college degree just to go work in a produce market? You know nobody's going to hire a Japanese engineer."

I felt like I'd been plugged into an electric light socket. I'd heard Cal say those things to his friends, but I'd never heard him talk like that to Mama and Papa.

"Aw, Cal," I said, "why'd you have to go and spoil everything?"

If Cal was giving up on being an engineer, I knew I might as well give up on being a teacher too.

Papa put his teacup down so hard the tea slopped out all over the table.

"California," he said. "Haven't I told you before there's nothing in the world more important for you now than getting a good education? Don't you realize that's the only thing that can bring you the kind of life your mama and I couldn't have? That's all we want from you, Cal. Not your money. Don't you see?"

Mama was nodding, but she was letting Papa do the talking.

I was surprised when Aunt Waka jumped into the conversation. "Why, California," she said, "you must never give up on a dream without even trying."

"What about Pa's dream?" Cal asked.

Aunt Waka didn't know what he meant, so Uncle Kanda told her about the garage and repair shop Papa'd always wanted. The two of them had their heads together in a conversation of their own. But Papa and Cal were still arguing back and forth at their end of the table.

"My dream can wait," Papa said to Cal, "but yours can't."

Mama was talking to Cal, but she looked at Joji and me. "You children must never lose hope," she said in a soft voice.

Finally Cal said, "Well, I'll think about it."

But he didn't say one way or the other what he was going to do. The whole day was spoiled now, like a brand new toy that got dropped in the mud. And nobody seemed to be able to think of anything cheerful to say.

That's when Joji spoke up. He'd been sitting as quiet as a doorknob during most of dinner. But suddenly he said, "I think I'll put Maxie outside tonight to guard the house."

"Do you really and honestly and absolutely mean it this time?" I asked him.

"I really mean it," Joji said. "In fact, I'm gonna put his box outside right now."

I guess maybe he was trying to do something to show he could help Mama and Papa too. So when Joji got up from the table, I said I'd help him, and I got up to go with him because I certainly didn't want to sit there and listen to any more arguing between Papa and Cal.

IX

◆ ◆

JOJI AND I CARRIED MAXIE'S BOX OUTSIDE AND
put it down beside the back steps.

"You be a good watchdog now," Joji told him,
"and bark good and loud if anybody comes sneaking
around. OK?"

Maxwell wagged his tail and sagged down into the
folds of all that skin hanging around his neck. I had
a kind of creepy feeling when we left him out there by
himself. In fact, I almost said something to Joji, but
I didn't. And now I keep wishing I had.

When I went to bed that night, I did my stretching
exercises. What I do is lie on my stomach and hook
my toes over the bottom edge of the mattress. Then I
reach up and grab the top end with my hands. I figure that might help me grow enough to catch up with
Tami one of these days. And if it does, it would be
worth all the knee aches I have to put up with. I said
my prayers next, which I can do in two minutes (I'm

not like Mama), and went to sleep.

I was in the middle of a really good dream about Tami and me being allowed to go swimming at the Crystal Plunge when I heard Maxie barking. He got all mixed up in my dream, and I was telling him they certainly wouldn't let a dog go in when they'd only gotten around to letting Tami and me in. But Maxie kept on barking, and pretty soon I got him sorted out from my dream and woke up.

I looked over at Joji, but he was sound asleep with all his covers thrown off. I stuck out my leg and poked him with my big toe. I was careful to pull my foot back in a hurry so he wouldn't bite my toe like he did once.

"Hey, Joji," I whispered. "Maxie's barking."

It took a lot more poking to finally wake him up. When he heard Maxie barking too, he scrambled out of bed and got his baseball bat from the closet.

"I'll git him, whoever's out there," he said.

I knew he was trying to act brave. But I knew Joji couldn't do anything alone, so I charged right through Aunt Waka's room and went to get Papa and Cal.

Papa was already up, getting into his bathrobe, and Mama was right behind him. By that time we were making such a commotion Aunt Waka and Cal were up too. We all followed Papa to the back door, and Cal grabbed the bat from Joji.

"Here, let me have that thing," he said. "I'll handle

whoever's out there."

"Be careful," Mama whispered.

Papa unlatched the screen door without making a sound. Just when he swung it open, there was a sound like a car backfiring, then footsteps running and a car driving off.

"Papa!" I yelled, and I grabbed his bathrobe.

But Papa pulled away from me and ran outside with Cal toward the garage. I heard Cal drop the bat and cry out, "Oh, no!"

We all rushed outside then, and there was poor Maxie lying in the driveway with blood pouring from his neck. Papa was bent over him trying to see if he had a pulse, and Cal had run out to the street to see if there was any sign of the car.

Joji put Maxie on his lap and kept stroking his head. "Aw, Maxie," he said, and he began to sob. "Don't die, Maxie. Please don't die."

But we all knew it was too late. Somebody had shot Maxie and not all of Joji's tears or even Aunt Waka's herbs and medicines could save him.

I began to cry too because I felt so bad. I wished I hadn't said all those mean things about Joji's dog. I wished I'd said something when I'd had that creepy feeling and told Joji not to leave Maxie outside.

Mama and Papa tried to comfort Joji, and Aunt Waka put her arm around me. She told me to stop crying, but I just couldn't.

Mrs. Sugar must have heard all the noise, because pretty soon she came padding over in her pink bathrobe and slippers.

"What is it?" she asked. "What's happened?"

Then she saw Joji with blood all over his pajamas, holding Maxie on his lap. She knelt down beside him and said, "Oh, my poor sweet Joji, who's done this awful thing to your darling Maxie?"

That was when Papa said what we were all thinking. "It must be more of Wilbur Starr's doing," he said, shaking his head. "I never thought he would do anything so cruel."

Papa's fists were clenched tight, and he looked angry and sad, as though he wanted to cry too.

Mrs. Sugar and Cal both thought Papa should call the police, but Papa said that wouldn't do any good.

"How can we prove it was Wilbur Starr's doing?" he asked.

And he was right. He said what we had to do was to bury Maxie. So Joji picked a spot in the corner of our backyard where Maxie used to bury his bones, and Cal helped Papa dig a big hole.

Mama wrapped Maxie up in an old sheet, and we all helped cover him up with the dirt he liked digging in. I picked a bunch of nasturtiums growing along the back fence, and I sprinkled them over the top of Maxie's grave.

Mama stayed out there with Joji after the rest of us

had started back inside. She patted the mound, like she was patting Maxie's head, and I heard her say, "Rest in peace, Maxwell. You were a good brave dog." It was like she was giving him a little funeral.

Then she made Joji come in, and she invited Mrs. Sugar to come have some cocoa with us. We all sat around the kitchen table, and I saw Cal put his arm around Joji. He hardly ever does that, but I guess he knew how much Joji was hurting. I wanted to do something too, but I was feeling just about as bad as Joji himself. No one said much, and it was Aunt Waka who finally began to talk.

"I still don't understand why this big laundry does so many terrible things to drive you out of business," she said. "Is your small laundry such a threat to them?"

Nobody answered her, so I said, "It's like I said, Aunt Waka. It's because we're Japanese and they hate us. Isn't it, Papa?"

Mrs. Sugar took my hand and squeezed it hard.

"It's only the fools and the bigots like Wilbur Starr who hate you," she said.

But I was still waiting for Papa to answer.

Papa leaned back in his chair and took a deep breath, like he was going to tell us a long story. He talked first in Japanese and then in English, so both Aunt Waka and Mrs. Sugar could understand.

Then he told how all this hatred began a long time

ago when the Japanese first came to America. He said they were called "heathens" and "Yellow Peril," and people threw rocks and horse manure at them when they walked down the streets. There were laws passed that kept more of them from immigrating to America and that kept them from owning land or becoming citizens once they got here.

"Imagine!" Mrs. Sugar said. She was shaking her head and making soft clucking sounds with her tongue.

"*Mah*, I never realized it was so bad," Aunt Waka whispered. She was sitting up very straight and stiff in her chair and leaning toward Papa so she wouldn't miss a word.

Papa had more to tell.

"You know, one of the first things I saw when I arrived in 1918 was a big billboard that said, 'Japs keep moving. This is a white man's neighborhood.' I'll never forget how I felt when I saw that," he said. "I'd always thought everybody had a fair chance in America. I'd come here with so many hopes and dreams. But that was only the first disappointment. There were many more."

I'd never heard Papa talk like that before. It was like he'd turned himself inside out and was showing us all the hurt that had been inside of him for so long.

Then Papa looked at Cal. "You know," he said, "in spite of everything, we never gave up. The more we were despised, the harder we worked. We always had hope that some day things would be better. If not for us, then for our children."

I knew Papa loved America even if it didn't love him back. He always hung out a big American flag on the Fourth of July and said some day if they'd ever let him, he was going to become an American citizen.

"Papa's right, you know," Mama said to Cal. "Now maybe we are stronger than all those people who hate us."

Aunt Waka suddenly stood up, like she was going to give a speech. "Of course, you are stronger," she said. "Of course, you are. And you must make that miserable creature—that Mr. Wilbur Starr—understand that." Then she sat down.

Aunt Waka kept surprising me all the time. I thought Japanese ladies were quiet and never spoke up, but Aunt Waka always did. She kept asking why or why not. I wondered what it was that made her seem so different from Mama or me. I certainly couldn't picture her ever wanting to shrink down into the sidewalk like I do.

Mama seemed surprised too. "Oh, Waka," she said, "how can we possibly make Wilbur Starr understand?"

"Why, just go over there and tell him to his face," she answered.

I thought that was a crazy idea. "He'd throw us out in a minute if we did that," I said. "He might even shoot us."

But Mrs. Sugar didn't think it was so crazy. "I'll wager if you ever met Wilbur Starr face to face, you'll find he's not only a bigoted fool, but a bully and coward as well."

Cal said she was probably right.

"Only a coward would come sneaking around at night and kill an innocent dog."

"We oughta go bash in his head," Joji growled.

Papa was sitting quietly, listening to everybody and rubbing the back of his neck.

Finally he said, "Maybe you're right, Waka. Maybe it is time for me to go have a talk with Wilbur Starr. I'll sleep on it and talk to Kanda about it tomorrow."

I didn't think Uncle Kanda would know what to do anymore than Papa. But maybe he was wiser than I thought.

It was starting to get light outside by then, and I could already hear the birds beginning to sing. I felt numb and unreal, as if everything that happened that night was an awful nightmare.

Pretty soon Mrs. Sugar went flapping back home in her pink slippers, and we all went back to bed. But I kept thinking about what Aunt Waka had said we should do. And I wondered what would happen if Papa really did go talk to Wilbur Starr.

I halfway wanted him to go and give him a piece of his mind. But I also didn't want him to go, because I was really scared. I was scared for Papa, and I was scared for the rest of us too.

X

IT WAS A GOOD THING THE NEXT DAY WAS SUN
day, because Papa had the whole day to think things
over and talk to Uncle Kanda. By the time Cal had to
leave for Stockton, Papa had made up his mind.

"Waka is right," he said. "It's time to make Wilbur
Starr understand he's never going to force us to give
up our laundry."

"You're going to confront him, then?" Cal asked.

"Tomorrow morning," Papa said. "And Kanda is
going with me."

"Well, good luck," Cal said. "I wish I could stay
and go with you."

But Papa answered, "There's only one thing I want
you to do, Cal, and I think you know what that is."

"I know," Cal said. But he still didn't say he'd do
it.

Mama was the one most worried.

She kept saying to Papa, "I think it's too dangerous for you and Mr. Kanda to go see Mr. Starr. Suppose he tries to harm you? Suppose he points a gun at you this time?"

But Aunt Waka told Mama we have to be willing to take chances sometimes when we know we're right.

"There comes a time," she said, "when you have to be strong and stand up for yourself."

It was as though Aunt Waka, just come from Japan, could see things we couldn't see for ourselves. As if we were in a glass box and she could see us from outside. She could see that Mama and Papa were really strong, but they'd been pushed down too long to realize it themselves. I guess she sort of gave them a push to do what she knew they could do.

But I felt more like Mama. I was worried and scared. What if those big burly drivers of the Starr Laundry trucks ganged up on Papa and Uncle Kanda and beat them up? What if somebody pulled out a gun and shot them this time?

By the time Papa left to go pick up Uncle Kanda the next morning, I knew what I had to do. I told Mama I was going next door to see Mrs. Sugar, but I didn't.

Instead I headed straight for Shattuck Avenue and the Starr Laundry. I was walking kind of slow, trying to build up my courage and wondering just what I was going to do once I got there. I really didn't know for sure. All I knew was that I had to be there so I could go for help if Papa and Uncle Kanda needed it.

I felt as if all the blood in my body was up in my face and the muscles in my neck were twitching. I'd only gone about a block when I heard somebody running behind me.

"Hey, Rink, wait for me."

It was Joji trying to catch up. And he had his baseball bat.

"You'd better not try anything funny with that," I warned him.

But Joji didn't listen. "He killed Maxie," he said, and he began to run.

I had to run to keep up with him, and pretty soon my knees began to ache, and even my elbows. I had a hard time swallowing, but I kept on running.

When we got to Shattuck Avenue, I could see the Starr Laundry across the street, and thank goodness, all the delivery trucks were out. At least the drivers weren't there to do something awful to Papa, I thought.

When we got closer, Joji began to slow down. Then he looked at me and said, "Now what'll we do, Rink?"

I certainly didn't know myself, but I kept on going. When we got to the laundry, I scrunched down low and peeked in through the plate glass window to see if Papa and Uncle Kanda were there. They were there, all right.

Papa had his hands pressed down on the counter and was leaning toward a tall thin man with mud-colored hair and steel-rimmed spectacles on his nose. He wore an eyeshade and black sleeve protectors, looking as if he'd been working on his books.

"That's him," I whispered to Joji. "That's old Wilbur Starr."

He looked just as mean as the day he'd yelled at us when we'd gone by his laundry.

The front door was open, and I crept closer so I could hear what was going on. Joji was right behind me. Papa was in the middle of a sentence, and all I heard was, ". . . and we have as much right to make a living in the laundry business as you have, Mr. Starr."

"After all," Uncle Kanda added, "you do not own the entire city of Berkeley."

I saw that Uncle Kanda was wearing his Sunday suit and his good black tie. He had his hat too, but he'd taken it off and was turning it around and around in his hands.

Wilbur Starr just glared at Papa and Uncle Kanda. Then he said, "You people are all alike, undercutting us with your cheap labor and cheap prices. That's bad for all of us. Why don't you just go on back where you came from?"

I felt like I'd been slapped in the face. I stepped back and squashed Joji's toe.

"Ow," he said, and he poked me with his baseball bat.

But I was too worried about Papa to have a fight then with Joji. I'd never heard anybody talk to Papa like that, and I thought sure he'd lose his temper and yell at Wilbur Starr and do something that would get him in real trouble.

But Papa didn't yell at all. He just straightened up real tall, and when he answered, his voice was like taut steel wire cutting into Mr. Starr's soft white flesh.

"Yes, we Japanese work hard," he said. "But there's no law against hard work is there? Suppose we do charge a little less than you? How can our small laundry ever be a threat to you, with four trucks picking up laundry all over the city?"

"Why are you so afraid of a little honest competition, Mr. Starr?" Uncle Kanda asked. "Aren't we all free in this country to pursue a livelihood?"

Uncle Kanda certainly was no dormouse today. I was surprised at the way he spoke up.

As soon as Uncle Kanda stopped, Papa went on. He was talking as if he was the main speaker at the Japanese Association picnic, standing on the platform with the red and white bunting and addressing a big crowd of people. He sounded like he'd never stop, and by then I was so scared, I could feel my heart pounding in my mouth and ears.

"You'd better stop now, Papa," I said, "or Mr. Starr's going to pull out his gun for sure."

But of course Papa couldn't hear me, and he kept

right on going. He asked Wilbur Starr what kind of human being he was to kill an innocent dog.

"I'm here to tell you, Mr. Starr," he said, "we are never giving up. You've only made us more determined than ever to keep our laundry going."

I looked at Wilbur Starr and saw his mouth was open, but no words were coming out. His eyes bulged, and he took off his eyeshade and wiped his forehead. Until now he'd always thrown a lot of hateful words at us and watched us run. But Papa hadn't run. He and Uncle Kanda had told him exactly what they thought of him, and Wilbur Starr looked like he'd run clean out of words. I knew then that Mrs. Sugar and Aunt Waka were right.

I felt like clapping for Papa and Uncle Kanda, I was so proud of them. I wanted to yell and cheer and turn cartwheels and throw fire crackers at the sun.

Instead I fell flat on my face, right in the doorway of the Starr Laundry because Joji had kept pushing from behind so he could see better. When I fell, Joji fell on top of me, and the two of us landed with a terrible racket right in front of everybody.

That was when Wilbur Starr finally found some words to say.

"Get outta here, you damn no-good Jap kids!" he screamed, and he came running from behind the counter with his hand raised in a big fist.

I ducked because I was sure he was going to hit Joji

and me. But Papa grabbed his arm before he could get near us.

"Don't you ever talk to my children like that again," Papa said real slow, making every word count. "And don't you or your men ever bother us again."

"Or next time," Uncle Kanda warned him, "you will be the one to be sorry."

Papa pulled Joji and me to our feet and said, "Come along, children, we're finished here."

Then he and Uncle Kanda just went striding down the street with their heads held high, and they never looked back once.

I did, though. I turned for one quick look at Wilbur Starr. His mouth was hanging open like a sick dog's, and he looked like he'd just swallowed a mouthful of hot chili and didn't know what to do with his face.

I knew I'd remember that look on his face as long as I lived. And I also knew then I'd never be afraid of him again. None of us would.

XI

WHEN MAMA HEARD WHAT HAPPENED AT THE Starr Laundry, she didn't even get mad at Joji and me for going there. She wiped her hands on her apron and kept asking, "Did your Papa really say all that to Mr. Starr? Did he really?"

Joji and I nodded.

"You should've seen the look on old Wilbur Starr's face," I said.

"Yeah, old prune face was really surprised. I could've bashed him on the head with my bat, except Rink got in my way," Joji bragged.

"I did not, Joji Tsujimura, and you know it. You were hiding behind me all the time. It was *you* who pushed and made me fall!"

"I did not. You fell all by yourself."

I guess Joji and I could have gone on for quite a while if Aunt Waka hadn't interrupted.

"*Mah,* I wish I could have been there too," she

said. "It must have been quite a sight, and I'm sure Mr. Starr will never bother you again."

"He's not going to scare me any more either," I said.

I marched into the bedroom and looked at myself in the mirror to see if I looked different. I felt so good after what happened at the Starr Laundry, I was sure I'd changed somehow. Maybe I'd even grown a little. I stood up real straight without slouching, and I looked at myself for a long time. Just then I felt like I could do almost anything.

From that day on, everything in my mind was either B.W.S (Before Wilbur Starr), or A.W.S (After Wilbur Starr), sort of like B.C. and A.D. in history.

"After Wilbur Starr," Papa seemed to feel better about everything too. He didn't even seem worried that business was getting worse at his barbershop. He just hung the "closed" sign on his door and spent more and more time helping Mama with the laundry. And when he wasn't doing that, he worked on fixing up old cars in the lot behind his shop.

When Mama worried about the rent and all the bills piling up again, he just said, "Don't worry, Mama. Everything will work out."

"How?" Mama wanted to know. "Am I supposed to start growing dollar bills on my tomatoes and cucumbers?"

"Maybe the chickens are going to start laying

golden eggs," I said.

But Papa just told us to be patient.

"I have an idea percolating in my head," he said, "and I'll tell you about it soon."

Sundays are the days when Big Things happen at our house. Sunday is sort of like a piece of bright gold brocade lying in a pile of white muslin weekdays. It's the day we wait for all week, when we put on our good Sunday clothes and go to church. If Mama is careful not to spend too much during the week, we have a nice dinner on Sunday. And if the chickens lay enough eggs, she bakes a sponge cake, her specialty, for dessert.

Sunday is also the day Uncle Kanda comes for dinner, and Tami too, if her mother will let her. So it's just an all-around special day. Naturally, it was on a Sunday, right after dinner, that Papa told us about his big idea.

"I've been thinking . . ." he began.

Joji immediately asked to be excused and had already started from the table when Papa said, "I want you to hear this too, Joji."

I knew then it was going to be something important. But I also knew it wasn't bad news, because Papa was smiling and looking pleased with himself.

Uncle Kanda took one more piece of yellow pickled radish, and I could hear his false teeth clicking as he

95

crunched on it between sips of tea.

"I'm listening," he said, so Papa wouldn't wait for him to finish eating before he went on.

By then I was sitting on the edge of my seat. I could hardly wait to hear about Papa's great new idea.

But he turned to Aunt Waka and said, "Before I tell you what's on my mind, I want to say, Waka, that I have *you* to thank for what I'm about to say. It was you who helped me find the courage to confront Wilbur Starr and speak up for my rights . . . to realize I'm strong enough to seek my dreams . . . to become my own man."

Good grief, I thought. Papa was making another speech the way he does at church or at a Japanese Association meeting.

"Hurry up, Papa," I said.

I wanted to go call Tami because I had a dozen things to tell her, even though I'd just seen her at church.

So Papa finally said, "What I want to do is close my barbershop."

"You what?" Mama asked, and she clutched at her chest.

Papa went right on as though he hadn't just about caused Mama to have a heart attack.

"We told Cal not to give up his dreams, and yet I realized that's what I almost did myself. It's just as Waka said, there comes a time when we have to take a chance or risk losing our dreams forever. I'd like to try opening my own garage and repair shop now, right here in our own garage. It's what I've always wanted to do."

Papa finally stopped and looked at Mama. "Well, what do you think?"

I never heard such a commotion as when Papa finally stopped. Everybody began to talk all at once. I could hear Mama, the worrier, say, "But won't that cost a lot of money, Papa? You'll need equipment and tools and . . ."

"I can sell my equipment at the barbershop," Papa answered. "And I already have some tools."

I also heard Aunt Waka say, "You can do it, Shintaro San. At least you must try, or you'll never know whether you can or not."

Uncle Kanda had finished eating his pickles at last and was just sitting there wiping his glasses with a rumpled up handkerchief. Papa looked at him, waiting for him to say something. And what Uncle Kanda said next was as much of a surprise as this great new idea of Papa's.

"Could you use a partner?" he asked Papa.

"You mean yourself?"

Papa looked like he was wondering how to tell Uncle Kanda he didn't exactly need a tailor for a partner in his new garage.

"Oh, I'm not saying I want to give up my own

work," Uncle Kanda said. "I just want to invest some money in your new garage to show my faith in you. For a long time I've been saving money for my old age, but I think it is better to be part of your big new dream right now."

Uncle Kanda grinned at Papa. "After all," he said, "we've shared a lot since we crossed the Pacific together, old friend, and I'd like nothing more than to be part of your new venture."

Suddenly, before Papa could say anything, Uncle Kanda got up and hurried to the bathroom. I thought it was a rather peculiar thing for him to do after making such a tremendous offer. But I supposed he just couldn't wait.

In a few minutes he came back carrying a long white cloth that looked like some sort of wide belt. When he laid it on the table, I could see it was stuffed with money folded up neat and flat in several pockets. Tami's mother was right, I thought. He *did* wear a money belt, and he *did* carry his life's savings wrapped around his stomach every minute of the night and day.

I realized then that Uncle Kanda had gone to the bathroom to take off his money belt, and he put it on the table to show Papa he really meant what he said. He pulled out a wad of bills from one of its pockets and spread out a handful of twenty dollar bills. He counted out five hundred dollars and put it in front of Papa.

"There," he said. "That should be enough to get you started in your new business."

Papa was so surprised, he was speechless. He just sat there blinking and looking back and forth at Uncle Kanda and the money. Finally he grabbed Uncle Kanda's hand and shook it a dozen times.

"That settles it," he said. "With your support, old friend, I know I can do it. We'll do it together. We'll call it the Kanda-Tsujimura Garage and Repair Shop, and I promise you, you'll never regret being a partner."

Papa and Uncle Kanda were beaming at each other, and I knew then why they were such good friends. They really cared about each other, and I guess they trusted each other too.

Mama was blinking hard and had to go find a handkerchief.

"*Mah*, Mr. Kanda, what can we say?" she asked. "How can we thank you?"

Aunt Waka didn't say anything, but she was nodding and smiling, and I could tell she was really pleased.

I looked at Joji, and his eyes were bulging. I guess mine were too. We'd never seen so much money all at once in all our lives. And the amazing thing was, there still seemed to be some left in Uncle Kanda's money belt.

I just couldn't wait another minute. I excused myself and went to phone Tami. I wanted to tell her that maybe her Mama had been right about Uncle Kanda being a miser before, but he certainly wasn't any more.

I was thinking that "After Wilbur Starr" even Uncle Kanda had changed too. Either that, or maybe it was just that I never really knew him before.

XII

◆◆◆◆◆◆◆◆◆◆◆◆◆◆◆◆◆◆◆◆◆◆◆◆

I'VE ALWAYS THOUGHT OUR GARAGE LOOKED like an orphan that didn't quite belong to anybody. When we first moved in, it was covered with ivy that hung from its roof in long tangles, like hair that needed one of Papa's haircuts. It also leaned to one side, looking like a strong gust of wind could just topple it over until Papa and Cal shored up its walls.

Papa chopped off the ivy and fixed up the inside with shelves and counters and called it his workshop until he got his Model T. Then it became his garage.

But after Papa decided on his great new plan, it became the Kanda-Tsujimura Garage and Repair Shop. Papa painted a huge sign, which he hung over the garage door, and moved his car out of the way to make room for all the business he expected to have.

Mrs. Sugar was his first customer. As soon as she saw Papa hammer up his sign, she rushed over with an old table radio under her arm.

"Do you repair radios as well as cars, Mr. Tsuji-mura?" she asked him.

"I repair anything that needs fixing," Papa told her. "And for you, there's no charge."

"Ah, you'll never get rich doing that," Mrs. Sugar warned.

But Papa really didn't care about getting rich. He just wanted to stay out of debt and make enough to feed us and keep Uncle Kanda from being sorry he'd become his partner.

Mama didn't care about getting rich either. She just wanted Papa to be able to pay his bills. And she decided she was glad Papa got rid of the barbershop after all, so he could finally do something he'd always wanted to do.

"It'll be nice to have you close by, too," she told him. "When summer's over and Waka and Rinko won't be here to help me, maybe you could give me a hand with some of the washing and rinsing."

"You bet," Papa told her. "I'll make up for both of them."

I didn't want to think about summer coming to an end. I wasn't looking forward to going back to school, and I certainly didn't want Aunt Waka to leave.

Mama didn't want to think about her leaving either, but she went over the list of places where she'd planned to take Aunt Waka and said, "Why, we haven't taken Waka to Golden Gate Park in San Francisco yet."

Papa said she certainly couldn't leave without seeing our famous park or the Cliff House where she could see Seal Rock.

"And don't forget the zoo," Joji reminded him.

"Oh, Joji," I said, "Aunt Waka doesn't want to go see a bunch of wild animals stuck behind bars."

But she said she'd like that. Actually, I think she was just being nice to Joji because of what happened to Maxie. So then I said, well, in that case, it was OK with me too.

At least the zoo was better than a circus. I hate seeing animals all dressed up and walking on their hind legs trying to look like human beings. If I had my way, I'd take all the circus animals in the whole world back to wherever they came from and let them out of their cages to run free forever.

Whenever we went anywhere besides our Japanese church, Mama lent Aunt Waka one of her dresses and dressed her up in a hat, gloves, shoes and stockings. Thank goodness she did, because I knew if Aunt Waka went walking around in her kimono everybody would glare at her, and somebody would probably tell her to go back where she came from.

I told Aunt Waka she really looked nice in western clothes, but I could tell she didn't like wearing them.

"They make me feel uncomfortable," she said, "as though I were somebody else and not me."

Since we were going to San Francisco on a Sunday, I naturally thought Uncle Kanda would be going with us, and I knew he'd like the picnic lunch Mama packed for us to eat at the park. We'd pick a nice isolated spot where no one would see us eating riceballs and pickles with our chopsticks.

When we went to pick him up for church though, Uncle Kanda wasn't waiting in front of his shop as he usually was, wearing his good black suit and his gray hat.

Papa told Joji to go up the back stairs and knock on his door. But when Joji came back down, he said Uncle Kanda wasn't home, and he'd found a note tacked to the door.

"That's odd," Papa said, when he read it. "All he says is that he's had to go out of town."

"Without telling us?" Mama asked. "That's not like him at all."

"Perhaps it was something urgent," Aunt Waka said. And then almost as if she knew where he'd gone, she said, "I'm sure he's quite all right."

But I could tell Mama wasn't so sure. She wasn't really listening when I asked if Tami could go with us to San Francisco in place of Uncle Kanda. She just nodded and said of course without giving it much thought. And that was how Tami happened to go with us to San Francisco that Sunday.

When we got to the zoo, Joji wanted to go to the Reptile House. But I certainly wasn't about to go near that awful place to see those slithering snakes, and neither were Tami or Aunt Waka. So the three of us went to see the elephants and Mama and Papa went with Joji. I was watching one of the elephants sniff up a peanut with his trunk when I heard Tami say to Aunt Waka, "Don't you want to stay in California forever?"

Aunt Waka smiled at her. "I'd certainly like being able to see you and Rinko whenever I liked."

"Well, you could if you married Uncle Kanda and stayed in California," Tami blurted out.

I gave Tami a really good poke with my elbow. She was acting just like her meddling mother.

I saw Aunt Waka blush and look like she'd swallowed a hot marshmallow. But in a minute she collected herself and said, "Why, Tami, is that what you hope for me?"

Tami had to drag me into it.

"Uh-huh," she said. "Me and Rinko both. And Mama too."

"Mostly her mama," I said real fast.

Aunt Waka nodded like she understood exactly how it was, and she brushed a hair from my face as if she wanted to show me she wasn't annoyed.

"Why, that's very kind of all of you," she said.

"But you see, my place is in Japan where my husband and son are buried and where Rinko's grandparents live. And most important, where I can be my true self."

When she said that, I thought about Mama's Japanese self locked up in her trunk, and I knew that's what Aunt Waka had that Mama had lost. I knew what Aunt Waka meant, but Tami didn't.

"Can't you be your true self in Berkeley?" she asked.

Aunt Waka led us over to a bench and sat down so she could rest her feet. Mama had stuffed some cotton into the toes of her shoes so Aunt Waka wouldn't walk right out of them, and I could tell Aunt Waka's feet were aching. She didn't complain, but every time she had a chance, she sat down, slipped off Mama's blue shoes, and wriggled her toes.

I'd taken a good look at her feet before to make sure neither one was deformed, but whenever she took off her shoes, I checked again to make sure.

"Does your foot hurt?" I asked her.

"Oh, no, not really," Aunt Waka said. "It's just that my feet aren't used to being squeezed into shoes. I have to let my toes out and give them a chance to wriggle once in a while." She covered her mouth with her hand and laughed at herself.

Tami and I sat down with her, and Tami just wouldn't let up.

"Why can't you?" she asked again.

I was sure she wanted to know why Aunt Waka couldn't marry Uncle Kanda. But Aunt Waka chose to say why she couldn't stay in Berkeley.

"I just don't think I could live in a land where I was always looked upon as a foreigner, unwanted and thought not to be as good as everyone else."

"But Mama and Papa have," I said.

"Yes," Aunt Waka said, "because they are strong. They've endured because they have patience and courage, Rinko. And they've managed to hold on to their Japanese selves."

I was surprised to hear Aunt Waka say that, because I'd been thinking all along they'd lost that. I also thought *she* was the one who was brave and strong. But maybe it really was Mama and Papa who were the brave ones after all.

Tami was still thinking about Uncle Kanda.

"I wonder where Uncle Kanda went today?" she asked. "And why would he just go off without telling anybody."

"I think maybe he just had something important he wanted to do," Aunt Waka said. And she pushed her feet back into Mama's shoes and brushed the dust from her dress.

"Come along, girls," she said. "Let's go look for the others."

* * *

That night after Joji and I were both in bed, I heard the telephone ring. The doors to Aunt Waka's room were still open, and I could hear Papa when he went to answer the phone. I'd just turned off my bed lamp and could still see the light inside my eyelids. I kept my eyes shut tight and concentrated on listening.

"Yes, yes," Papa was saying. "Are you sure? How did it happen? Ah . . . ah . . . yes. I'll come immediately."

I could tell by the sound of Papa's voice that it was something bad.

"Hey, Joji," I said in the dark.

I needed somebody to talk to. But Joji was already sound asleep, so I got out of bed and ran barefooted into the kitchen.

Papa was putting on his jacket and hat, and Mama was telling him to drive carefully.

"What happened?" I asked Papa. "Where're you going?"

"It's Uncle Kanda. He's in the hospital."

"You mean that's where he's been all day?"

"No, he was just hit by a car outside the bus depot."

Papa didn't have any more time to talk to me. He ran out the door, and I could hear him cranking up the car.

Mama immediately got the broom from the closet and began sweeping the kitchen floor. Whenever she's really worried, she either cooks something or cleans

108

house, because she can't sit still.

"What in the world was he doing down at the bus depot so late at night?" she asked the broom. "And with his bad eyes too. He probably didn't even see the car in the dark. Why didn't he call Papa? Why didn't he let us know where he was going?"

She was going on and on, sweeping harder and harder, pushing the broom under the stove and around its legs and around the table and all the chair legs gathered under it, trying to find some dust. She didn't even tell me to go back to bed.

Aunt Waka brought out the dust pan and held it for Mama so she could sweep what little dust there was into it. When she'd emptied it in the garbage can, she finally said, "I have a notion Mr. Kanda might have gone to Stockton today."

"Stockton? What for?" Mama asked.

"To talk to California. Mr. Kanda was very worried about him."

"Ah, all that talk about dropping out of college."

And then I remembered how Uncle Kanda and Aunt Waka'd had their heads together talking while Cal argued with Papa that day. That was probably why Aunt Waka knew where Uncle Kanda had gone.

"Mr. Kanda wanted to talk to California without your knowing," Aunt Waka said to Mama. "He said it was something between the two of them."

But Aunt Waka looked worried now, too. "I do

hope he's going to be all right."

It was all Cal's fault, I thought. If anything happened to Uncle Kanda just when he and Papa had finally decided to get their dream going, it would be because of Cal, the one Uncle Kanda loved best.

XIII

UNCLE KANDA WAS UNCONSCIOUS FOR TWO DAYS, and all that time Papa didn't even go near his garage. He spent each day at the hospital waiting for Uncle Kanda to come to. Mama did a lot of extra praying, and I did too, because I was afraid Uncle Kanda was going to die.

I thought how awful it would be if we had to bury him the way we'd buried Maxie, and I would never see him again, ever. I thought about all the Sundays he'd come for dinner and how brave he'd been the day he and Papa went to confront Wilbur Starr. I thought of all the good things I knew about him—especially how he'd helped when Papa needed him. I laid them out one by one inside my head so God could see them and would want to let him stay around a few more years.

Finally on the third day Papa came home looking tired but happy. He said Uncle Kanda was going to be

111

OK, and Mama immediately said she'd make some rice balls and soybean soup for Uncle Kanda.

"I know that's what he'd rather have than the meat and potatoes they'll give him at the hospital," she said.

Papa told us the first thing Uncle Kanda said to him was, "Where's the letter? What's happened to the letter?"

Papa thought he was delirious, but he wasn't. It turned out he'd gone to see Cal, just as Aunt Waka thought, and he'd brought back a letter from Cal for Mama and Papa.

Papa took the letter out of his pocket then and read it to us. It was only a few lines long.

Dear Ma and Pa, it said.

Uncle Kanda convinced me I was wrong. So I guess I'll be going back to the university this fall after all. What the heck, Pa, if you can open up your own garage, I guess I should try to be an engineer. Who knows, I may even get hired someday. I'll never know unless I try, will I? See you in September.

Love,
Cal

"Good for you, California," Aunt Waka said, as though he was sitting right there. "Good for Mr. Kanda, too."

Papa was grinning. "That's some partner I have, isn't it?" he asked. "Just think he went all the way to Stockton on the bus and actually talked some sense into Cal."

"Thank God," Mama said.

She probably would've had one of her long conversations with God right then and there if Aunt Waka and I hadn't reminded her we still had a big wash to do in the basement.

Papa had one more thing to tell us. He looked at me and said, "Kanda is asking to see you."

"Who, me?"

"That's what he said."

I couldn't imagine why Uncle Kanda would want to see me. And I wasn't so sure I wanted to go see him lying pale and sickly in a hospital. I hate going to hospitals as much as I hate going to the dentist. But Papa told me to go that afternoon.

"You can go by yourself on the streetcar, can't you, Rinko?" he asked. "I really should do some work in the garage."

"I guess so," I said, even though I really wanted Papa to go with me.

Mama immediately made plans of her own.

"Good," she said. "Then you can take him the soup and riceballs. I know they'll make him feel better."

When I was ready to go, I saw that Mama was about

to wrap the thermos and box of riceballs in the silk square she uses to carry her Bible and Japanese hymnal to church. So I immediately got a paper sack from the bag where Mama keeps her paper bags and used string.

"Here, Mama, use this instead," I told her.

I knew she'd say, "But a silk *furoshiki* looks so much nicer, Rinko."

And that is exactly what she said. Sometimes Mama just doesn't understand. I knew if I got on the street-car carrying a *furoshiki* bundle, everybody would stare at me as though I'd just gotten off a boat from Japan.

So I said, "Uncle Kanda won't care what it's wrapped in as long as the stuff inside tastes good."

Mama looked at me for a minute and then just said, "I suppose you're right, Rinko."

She put everything in the brown paper sack and told me to be careful not to drop the thermos.

Mama certainly didn't have to remind me. I don't know how many times I used to break the thermos in my lunch box when I was little. I never remembered dropping it or even banging it against anything. But when I went to the cloak room at noon to get my lunch box, it would be sitting there oozing out all the nice hot cocoa Mama had put in my thermos. I certainly didn't want that happening to me on the streetcar with the soybean soup.

Once when Mama and I were on the streetcar taking some vinegared rice and yellow pickled radish to a sick church friend, that radish smelled so bad nobody would sit near us. The conductor finally came back to open all the windows around us, and I was so embarrassed I wanted to crawl under the seat and disappear.

"Just pretend nothing is wrong," Mama said. "And sit up straight."

She stuffed the smelly radish down to the bottom of her shopping bag, but still I knew everybody on the streetcar could smell it. I could tell from all the dirty looks we got. I thought we'd never get to our stop, but we finally did, and I was never so glad as when we got off that streetcar.

I didn't have to tell Mama not to send over any pickled radish to Uncle Kanda. I guess she never forgot that streetcar ride either.

When I walked into the hospital, I began holding my breath. I don't know why. I certainly wasn't trying to become invisible. I guess I was just nervous. Or maybe I was trying not to inhale all the germs I thought must be wafting around from all those sick and dying people in the hospital.

I get scared when I think about dying and about how dark and black and final it must be. Then I try to remember the Heaven they tell us about at church and think it wouldn't be so bad if everybody ended up there and turned into angels. It's just that sometimes I'm not sure I'd qualify. And I certainly don't want to go to that other place.

I went up to a counter to ask the nurse where I could find Uncle Kanda. She glanced up at me, but kept on writing in a big notebook. Her blonde hair was marcelled just like Mrs. Phillips' and she had two circles of rouge on her cheeks too. I wondered if she fixed herself up like that every day just to go to work. Her face looked like it was going to a party and only the rest of her, all in white, looked like it belonged in a hospital.

The nurse didn't pay the slightest attention to me. But I was used to that. Sometimes at Judson's Department Store, the clerks wait on everybody else before they'll come wait on Mama and me. And if I ever go by myself, sometimes they ignore me completely.

The nurse made me think of Wilbur Starr. So I straightened up and took a big gulp of air and said in a loud, firm voice, "I want to see Mr. Manjiro Kanda right now, please."

I guess I surprised her, because I certainly surprised myself She looked up his room number right away then and told me where to find him.

Uncle Kanda was in a ward with five other men, and I was glad to see he had the bed by the window. A patch of sun was coming in and making a bright square on the blanket right where his hand was. I could see all the veins standing out bluish green on the back of his hand, and I saw that he had a big white bandage around his head. His eyes were closed, and he smelled of antiseptics and medicine, and I thought he must be dying.

I put the brown sack by his hand so he could feel it and then he opened his eyes.

"Hello, Uncle Kanda. It's me, Rinko. Does your head hurt?"

Uncle Kanda smiled at me, and I could see it was a real effort for him just to do that. "Not more than I can bear," he whispered.

I told him Mama had made him some soybean soup and riceballs, and he said that was very kind of her. And then he closed his eyes again. I thought for a minute he'd forgotten why he wanted to see me.

I didn't know what else to say to him, so I just stood there wriggling my toes and wishing he'd hurry up and tell me whatever it was he had to say. I wished Mama or Aunt Waka or even old Joji had come with me in case Uncle Kanda decided to die right then and there in front of me.

But finally he opened his eyes and said, "Still have your 'going to college' jar, do you?"

"Sure, Uncle Kanda."

"That's a good girl."

He closed his eyes again. Was that all, I wondered.

He just wanted to see me to ask that?

I touched his hand to keep him awake and said, "I have almost ten dollars in it now."

Uncle Kanda was having a hard time keeping his eyes open. His eyelids kept fluttering like the wings of a moth near a bright light, and I could see the milky rim around his eyeballs because he wasn't wearing his thick glasses.

"Your brother asked me to tell you something," he whispered at last.

"Cal? What'd he say?" I leaned closer so I could hear.

"He said . . . he said for you not to give up either. He said for you to be the teacher in the family, and he'd be the engineer."

"He said that?"

Uncle Kanda tried to give me a small nod. "You won't give up will you, Rinko?"

"Never," I said.

I said that because I wanted to make Uncle Kanda feel better, but I also meant it.

Ever since that day we went to see Wilbur Starr, I had this feeling sitting deep down inside me that I could do almost anything. It wasn't quite as strong as it'd been that day, but I knew it was still down there like a little mushroom, waiting to grow bigger one of these days.

Pretty soon a nurse came bustling in and told me

I had to leave. I told Uncle Kanda to get well soon, and he said he'd try, and he closed his eyes again.

"He's going to be all right, isn't he?" I asked the nurse.

She didn't say yes or no. She just said, "Don't worry, we'll take good care of him."

When I got home and told Mama and Aunt Waka what Uncle Kanda told me and what I said back, both their faces crinkled up into the same kind of happy smile.

Then Aunt Waka said, "That's good, Rinko. Now I can go home with my mind at rest."

"Go home? You're leaving already, Aunt Waka?"

It was only the middle of August, but Aunt Waka said she'd been here for over two months, and it was time now for her to go home.

"Will you do one thing for me before I go?" she asked.

By then I was ready to do anything for her. "Sure," I said.

"Will you put on the kimono I brought so I can take a picture of you in it for your Grandma and Grandpa?"

"I'll do it Sunday," I promised.

I'd do it on the day that Big Things happen at our house.

XIV

⬥◆⬥◆⬥◆⬥◆⬥◆⬥◆⬥◆⬥◆⬥◆⬥◆⬥◆⬥◆

A PROMISE IS A PROMISE, SO ON SUNDAY AFTER dinner, I got out the kimono Aunt Waka had brought me. It was in my bureau drawer still folded nice and flat inside its soft rice paper wrapping.

One good thing about kimonos is that they don't wrinkle if you fold them properly on the seams. Also almost anybody can wear the same size because there are no buttons or snaps. If you're short, you just pull up more to make a tuck and tie it in place with a silk cord. I thought that was pretty clever when Aunt Waka pointed it out to me.

She had to help me get dressed in the kimono because I certainly couldn't do it by myself. She made sure I overlapped the left side over the right (boys do the opposite), and she wound the wide brocade *obi* around and around my middle and tied an enormous knot in back.

I felt as if I was bound up in a silk cocoon and could hardly bend down to put the white *tabi* socks on my feet. It was hard to walk, too, with the thongs of the *zori*—the sandals—digging in between my toes, and I discovered why Aunt Waka took those small steps when she walked. You have to, with the long narrow kimono coming down to your ankles.

"There, you look beautiful," Aunt Waka said, when she'd finished. "Go look at yourself in the mirror."

I padded over in small steps to the bureau and looked at myself. I held out my arms to look at the white peonies blooming on the long blue silky sleeves. I turned around and twisted my head to look at the knot of the *obi* in back. I knew then exactly how Aunt Waka felt when we made her get into western clothes.

"That's not me," I said.

Aunt Waka smiled. "I know how you feel, but it's you all right."

Then she hurried me out to the parlor to show Mama and Papa how I looked.

Mama's eyes really lit up when she saw me. "Why, Rinko, you look so pretty." And then she said, "Stand up straight now." But she didn't say it the way she usually does in order to improve my posture. She said it as though she wanted me to feel proud of myself.

121

I guess Papa was about as pleased as Mama. He stood back and studied me as though he was taking a picture of me.

"I suppose you wouldn't consider going to the hospital to show Uncle Kanda how you look, would you? That would really cheer him up, you know."

"Never in a million years," I said.

So Papa told Joji to get the box camera he got for Christmas and take my picture for Uncle Kanda. Aunt Waka got her camera too. We all trooped outside, and I stood beside the peach tree squinting at the sun.

"Stop squinting, Rinky Dink," Joji said.

"Don't you call me that, Joji Tsujimura," I said. I raised my arm to give him a whack and that's when he took my picture.

"Smile," Aunt Waka said, focusing her camera.

I blinked, and that's when she squeezed the shutter.

Mama wanted a picture with all of us in it, so I went over to get Mrs. Sugar. She looked exactly the way I thought she would when she saw me wearing a kimono. Her mouth made a big O, but no sound came out.

Then she said, "Why, it's my sweet little Japanese Rinko," and she gave me a hug. But it was hard to hug her back being wrapped up like a package in all that stiff brocade.

Mrs. Sugar lined us up in front of Papa's garage

122

and made sure she got his big sign in the picture too.

"There," she said when she'd taken three pictures. "This will be a fine commemoration of your aunt's visit."

She sounded just like the people at church. They are always taking pictures to commemorate Easter or Memorial Day or somebody's baptism or even somebody's funeral.

I could hardly wait to get out of the kimono when we were finished with all the picture-taking. Aunt Waka untied and unwound everything, and I shook my bones loose to get my circulation going again.

"Boy, am I glad to get out of that thing," I said.

Then I remembered the kimono was a present from Aunt Waka, and I tried to think of something nicer to say.

"I'll have Mama put it in her trunk and cover it with mothballs," I said.

I guess that wasn't exactly what Aunt Waka wanted to hear either. I thought she probably would've liked me to say I'd get it out and wear it once in a while.

But she didn't say that. She just smiled and said, "Ah, Rinko, you certainly are a child of America." Then she turned serious and said, "But don't ever forget, a part of you will always be Japanese too, even if you never wear a kimono again."

"I know," I said. "It's the part that makes me feel different and not as good as the others."

It was the strangest thing. Suddenly, it was as if I'd opened a faucet in my head and everything inside came pouring out. I told Aunt Waka all about how I felt at school—how the boys called me names and the girls made me feel left out. And I told her a terrible secret I'd kept to myself and never told anybody, ever.

Once when there was going to be a PTA meeting at school and we had notes to bring home, I tore up my note and never gave it to Mama. I did it because I didn't want Mama to go. I didn't want her bowing to all my teachers and talking to them in the funny English she sometimes uses. I didn't want Mama to be ignored by everybody and left sitting in a corner. I guess maybe I was a little bit ashamed of Mama. But mostly I was ashamed of myself.

"I hate always being different and left out," I told Aunt Waka.

Aunt Waka was folding my kimono and *obi* on top of my bed, smoothing them out carefully so there would be no wrinkles. She wrapped them up again in the soft rice paper and tied them up just the way they were when she'd brought them. Then she put them aside and sat down on my bed.

"I think I understand how you feel, Rinko," she said in a soft whispery voice. "When I was young and couldn't run or play with my friends, they used to tease me and call me a cripple. They often made me cry."

I thought of the old photograph of Aunt Waka standing with the crutch. "But you were smiling anyway," I said, as if she'd know what I was remembering.

"Just because you're different from other people doesn't mean you're not as good or that you have to dislike yourself," she said.

She looked straight into my eyes, as if she could see all the things that were muddling around inside my brain.

"Rinko, don't ever be ashamed of who you are," she said. "Just be the best person you can. Believe in your own worth. And someday I know you'll be able to feel proud of yourself, even the part of you that's different . . . the part that's Japanese."

I was still in my slip sitting next to Aunt Waka and wriggling my toes as I listened to her. And then it happened, like a light bulb had been switched on in my head. At that very minute I finally knew what made Aunt Waka seem so special. She was exactly the kind of person she was telling me to be. She believed in herself and she liked herself. But mostly, I guess she was proud of who she was.

I hate saying good-bye to somebody I like, especially when I don't know when I'll ever see that person again. I didn't even want to think about saying good-bye to Aunt Waka.

She tried to cheer me up. "Who knows, Rinko," she said. "Maybe someday you'll come to visit me in Japan."

"I could start a 'going to Japan' jar," I said.

"Yes, it could be your 'jar of dreams.'"

I knew I couldn't do it until after I'd filled up my "going to college" jar. Maybe not even until after I'd finished college and become a teacher.

But Aunt Waka clasped her hands together and talked as though I might be coming next year.

"Wouldn't that be wonderful, Rinko?" she said. "I'll be waiting for you."

Mama stuffed Aunt Waka's willow basket with all kinds of presents for Grandpa and Grandma. She packed boxes of chocolate kisses and cube sugar and tins of coffee and bags of walnuts and a big white table cloth she'd crocheted. It was round and white and looked like a giant snowflake. She'd been working on it every night since before Aunt Waka came, and she finished it just in time for Aunt Waka to take home with her.

"What else can I send home with you?" Mama asked, looking around the house for something more. She probably would've put in a few dozen eggs and one of her sponge cakes if she could.

When the willow basket couldn't hold another thing, Papa tied it up and Aunt Waka packed away her small

Buddhist altar and all her clothes. Then she spent the last two days saying good-bye to everybody.

I went with her to see Uncle Kanda. He'd gone home now and was doing fine and only needed one of the church ladies to come make supper for him. He was sitting in a wicker chair with a blanket wrapped around his knees, and he certainly looked a lot better than when I saw him in the hospital. He told Aunt Waka, "This is one of the nicest summers I've ever had."

"Even if you cracked your head?" I asked.

"Yes, even with that."

"Perhaps you will come to visit your native land someday," Aunt Waka said to him.

Uncle Kanda looked off into the distance, as if maybe he was seeing the green rice fields in his old village.

"Perhaps someday," he said. But he didn't sound like he really meant it, and Aunt Waka didn't say she'd be waiting.

I had a strange feeling they'd probably never see each other again. But I could tell by the way they smiled at each other that they'd always be friends.

Aunt Waka said good-bye to Tami and her mother at church. I guess Aunt Waka never did mind going to church with Mama every Sunday, even if it wasn't a Buddhist temple. She just said faith was faith, whether we got it in church or in a temple. And she even learned the words to "Onward Christian Soldiers."

I guess Tami's mother was disappointed she hadn't been able to match Aunt Waka up with Uncle Kanda.

"You will be back one day, won't you?" she asked.

Aunt Waka said she certainly hoped so, and I guess Tami's mother thought she'd have another chance next time. But I knew better.

The night before Aunt Waka left, Mrs. Sugar invited us all to her house for dinner. It was the first time we all got invited together, and Mrs. Sugar used her best china and her plated silverware and baked a big ham.

She gave Aunt Waka a beaded coin purse and several hugs and said she might even go to Japan someday to visit her.

And Aunt Waka said, "I'll be waiting for you," just the way she said she'd wait for me.

The next morning Mama, Papa, Joji, and I took Aunt Waka to San Francisco to the same pier where we'd gone to meet her. Another big ship was berthed there, waiting to take her back to Japan.

Mrs. Sugar would've been surprised at all the hugging Aunt Waka and Mama and I did when it was time to say good-bye. And crying too, especially Mama.

When the ship was about to sail, the small band on

the first class deck played "Aloha Oe," and everybody threw pastel-colored streamers from the railing down to their friends on the pier. I was afraid the third class passengers wouldn't get any, but, thank goodness, they did.

Aunt Waka threw her first roll of colored tape to me. I guess because it was my favorite color, blue. Then she threw one each to Mama and Papa and Joji, so we each had a streamer linking us to Aunt Waka up there on the ship.

There must've been hundreds of pink and yellow and lavender and blue streamers all tangled up and billowing in the breeze. It was all so beautiful and sad, what with the music and all, I wanted to cry.

When the gangplanks were drawn up, the band played "Auld Lang Syne." Mama cried some more, and Papa held his streamer in one hand and waved his hat with the other.

"*Sayonara*, Waka . . . good-bye . . ." he was shouting.

"Take care of yourself," Mama called, but I don't think Aunt Waka heard her, because the ship's whistle gave three long blasts, and then it slowly began to pull away from the pier.

"Come on, Joji," I said, and we walked along the pier trying to keep up with the ship and make our streamers last as long as we could.

129

I could feel the roll of tape spinning on my finger, slowly at first and then faster and faster as the ship moved out to sea.

"So long, Aunt Waka. Come back!" Joji yelled.

He tried to wave, and his yellow streamer snapped and went flying off with the wind.

But I was still connected to Aunt Waka. She was like a kite flying way up in the sky, with only a thin piece of string to keep her linked up with me.

"I'll come see you in Japan!" I yelled as loud as I could.

Now that I couldn't talk to her, I thought of a million things I wanted to say to Aunt Waka. I wanted to tell her that this had been one of the best summers of my entire life, and that from then on I'd think of everything that happened to me as "Before Aunt Waka" or "After Aunt Waka," because *she* was the one who'd made the difference in our lives, not Wilbur Starr.

I guess Aunt Waka had stirred us up and changed us all so we'd never be quite the same again. I was really beginning to feel better about myself—even the part of me that was Japanese—and I almost looked forward to going back to school to see if maybe things would be different.

But it was too late to tell her. Aunt Waka was gone. All I could do was just stand there straight and tall, hoping Aunt Waka could still see me with my hand stretched up high over my head.

I stood there a long time watching Aunt Waka's ship going further and further away from me, until finally my blue streamer was all unrolled and went flying off into the summer sky.